Wreck

By

Stacey Brandon

&

Karen Bell

Wreck

Book Three in The Crash Series

Cover Designer/Photography
Stacey Brandon Photography

Editing
Donnie Bell

Design and Formatting
Tyler Bell

First Printing, 2016

ISBN 978-0-9967928-4-4

www.BrandonBellAuthors.com

First Edition

The Crash Series

Crash

Fall

Wreck

Coming Next

Lovely Deception

Dedications

We dedicate "WRECK"

to everyone with a dream

they refuse to give up on.

It CAN happen ;)

Contents

Chapter One: Kyle
Nothing To Talk About

Oh my God...Is Liv's kid eating his snot?

"Ben! No! Mommy says, NO!" I watch with disgust and amazement as the woman I've always considered the coolest person I know, swipes a ratty wad of tissue under her young son's nose and then shoves it into her own pocket.

Is that normal behavior for a new mom or does Liv just not give a shit about what anyone thinks? With her, my money is on the latter.

"Kyle!" My name barked from across the room gives me the perfect excuse to turn away before Liv notices my horror. I need some time to process how much my friend has changed. That change has reaffirmed my vow to skip the joys of fatherhood.

Ronan is standing near the backdoor, impatiently motioning for me to join him. Despite being my boss, and one of the most inflexible men I've ever met, he's my friend and I have to believe

1

he noticed my distress and came in for a save. It's appreciated and I don't need to be asked twice.

I sneak a glance at my watch as I maneuver around the smiling, chatting guests. What I'd believed to be several hours is revealed to be a sum total of forty-seven minutes. *How is that possible?*

'Come to our housewarming party,' they said. 'It will be fun,' they promised. Charli and Logan are damn liars. Okay, maybe that's not fair. They probably think that kind of shit is fun. They, like Liz, have changed a lot in the last couple of years. I should have known when my girl Charli hooked up with Logan it was the beginning of the end. I still adore her and always will, just like Liv, but we now reside in different worlds.

Back in the day, Charli and Liv were waitresses at Ronan's bar, *The Crash.* I was the bartender. Actually, I still bartend there, but I'm also the assistant manager. Our shifts together had cemented a friendship that nothing can shake. I consider these girls my family. That's why I'm here today, even though our nights of tequila shots and never-ending pool matches are a thing of the past.

A few years ago, Charli met Logan. What had originally seemed an unlikely pairing had actually worked out well. They got married, they bought a house, and now they are expecting their first kid.

Liv, thanks to Charli's wedding, had met Zac. Their relationship was a lot more complicated and she's the last girl to ever do things in a conventional way, hence her son arriving about eight months ago. She's just now planning on making an honest man out of his daddy.

The girls now have busy lives that have moved them in new directions. I'm still happily the same man I've always been...but I miss them and the crazy shit we got up to.

I won't admit it of course. My man card is already in danger of being revoked just for being at this damn housewarming party. *Why the fuck do you need to have a party to celebrate buying a house anyway?*

The door is finally within my reach. Surely the backyard and alcohol will be my salvation. Suddenly, I feel a hand slide around my arm.

"It's Kyle, right?" A soft, feminine voice and an insistent tug on my forearm force me to turn. I'm rewarded by the sight of a voluptuous brunette licking the edge of her cherry-red lips and leaning close enough to give me a generous view down her top. The green fabric of her dress, what little of it there is anyway, shimmers slightly with each breath she takes.

I smile. Maybe Ronan can wait another minute or two.

"That's right. I'm Kyle. Haven't we met?" I raise a single eyebrow, never taking my gaze from hers. It's a trick I picked up bartending. If we haven't met, she'll feel flattered that I'm reciprocating her interest. If we have met, and I've forgotten, the look lends just enough ambiguity where she'll think maybe I really do remember her, but I'm playing the game.

Her answering smile is all I need to see my gamble paid off. "Actually, we have... a few weeks ago, when you stopped by Zac's restaurant. I'm the hostess."

I do remember going to the restaurant. Zac had invited me to have a few drinks with him at closing one night when Liv was doing something with Charli. I vaguely recall the hostess as being attractive and Zac warning me against her. *What had he said?*

"Of course." I look at every inch of her, slowly taking in every detail. "I remember, exactly," I lie. "It's great to see you again." Is it, really? It should be. She's hot and obviously into me. She's

3

just the kind of woman I like. Just the kind of woman I need... to forget about the one I can't have.

Her giggle is light but seductive. "Well, I'm just here to drop off some extra serving utensils from the restaurant. I'm not actually friends with the hosts or anything." She leans even closer and drops her voice to almost a whisper. "It's a beautiful house and all, but this kind of party is not really my scene anyway. Doesn't seem like you're enjoying it too much either. Can you get away?"

It's tempting. It's more than tempting.

"I'd like to but..." I put a dose of regret in my voice and she pouts with sympathy.

"I understand. Maybe we could find something more...*interesting*... to do together later?" she asks, while slipping her hand into my back pocket and sliding out my phone. "I'll give you my number."

"Absolutely, sweetheart."

She hands back the phone and walks away, making sure to put a little extra swing in her step for my benefit. It's a beautiful sight.

"Damn" I breathe out. She might be exactly what I need right now. I look down at the now dark screen on my phone, realizing she never told me her name. I pull up my contacts, trying to figure out what the last number entered had been, but I can't tell which it was. There are far too many numbers to scroll through them all. How in the hell am I going to figure out who she is?

Shit, I'm going to have to track Zac down and ask him for his hostess's name. Maybe he can remind me why he warned me off her, even though I probably won't let it sway me.

Finally, I slip out the back door to find Ronan and Logan deep in conversation, standing near a stainless steel barbecue pit as big as my Grandma's '63 Buick LeSabre.

What is Logan going to cook on that thing? A dinosaur?

Ronan's eyes are glazing over as he listens to the over-en-thusiastic praise of the grill's shiny surfaces, the excellent deal Logan got on it since they were having an end-of-season sale, and exactly how many ribeyes the beauty can handle. Logan invol-untarily caresses the multiple knobs and buttons along the front reminding me of the bar patrons that come alone, have a few too many drinks and try to seal the deal before closing.

"She's a sure thing, you've already got her home, Logan. No foreplay required," I mutter under my breath, as I join them.

"What?" He shoots me a look of confusion.

"Nothing. Forget it."

He motions me closer. "Have you seen the grill yet, Kyle? Look under here at the custom cabinet to hold the propane bottle and…"

Shaking my head, I slap a hand on his back. "You are a lost cause." I take a good look at the silver monstrosity. "Dude… How many kids are you and Charli planning to pop out? You could use this thing to feed a small country."

"She's beautiful, isn't she?" Logan beams with no embarrass-ment.

Charli pokes her head out the back door and yells in our di-rection. "Hey, Ronan…Kinleigh is here!" Ronan, a military man through and through, lets his usually rigid posture melt a little at the mention of his daughter's arrival.

I, on the other hand, become a tight ball of tension as my gut seizes in panic. My instinct screams for me to run. I didn't know Kinleigh would be here. She isn't even supposed to be in town. I haven't seen her in months. I don't want to now.

I'm a fucking coward.

I watch Ronan's hulking form follow Charli back into the

house, obviously excited to find his daughter. *Had everyone else known to expect her? Had they chosen not to tell me?*

Looking back toward Logan and the oversized grill, I discover he is staring at me with... sympathy? *Shit. What does he think he knows?*

"So... Kinleigh is here," Logan says, testing the waters.

"Apparently." I take a long pull off my beer, even though I've been holding the bottle long enough for it to become lukewarm and unappealing.

"Charli might have mentioned that you and she..." Logan raises his eyebrows.

"Charli doesn't know what she's talking about. Nothing happened between Kinleigh and me." My fists clench at my side as I try to appear unaffected by his nosy-ass questions.

"Okay." Logan smirks. "If you say so, Kyle."

"I say so. Shut the fuck up and tell me about your grill, Logan." This is all the encouragement he needs to jump into a ten-minute speech about how many hot dogs the damn thing will hold for his future kids' birthday parties.

Several minutes later, I barely register the squeak of the patio's screen door opening behind me, until the breeze carries the strong scent of brown sugar and vanilla. The familiarity makes my stomach clench into a knot and my heart rate ratchets up to an uncomfortable pace.

She's here.

"Hey, Kyle." Soft and sweet, poured over confidence and determination, her voice slams against my resolve. I know firsthand she isn't timid when she wants something.

When I fail to respond, Logan claps his hands together loudly to break the silence. "I think I need another beer. Can I grab one for you, Kyle? Kinleigh?" Silence ticks by. "No? Okay, well then..."

His head swings back and forth between us like he's watching a tennis match.

"I'm good. Thanks," I finally tell Logan, determined to keep this from becoming any more awkward. My efforts are probably wasted though when my back is still firmly facing her and I haven't even acknowledged her arrival. It's just that I know, once I turn around... there will be no escape.

"Yeah..." Logan lets his voice trail off as he leaves us alone.

I can hear the tapping of her shoe beating out a steady, quick rhythm on the patio pavers. "Kyle?" Her voice drips with agitation.

It's time to man up.

Slowly, I turn. Raising my eyes to meet hers, I'm disappointed in my reaction but not surprised. A jolt of hot desire hits me like a sucker punch. Easily the most beautiful woman I've ever known, she always has this effect on me, regardless of how many times I'm around her. I'm convinced I'll go the rest of my life without ever seeing her equal.

Her hair is referred to as blonde, but that's too simple a description. It is pale gold and platinum and reflects every visible color when the light hits it just right. Her eyes are the Pacific Ocean on a clear day. Twin dimples flank her generous mouth and full lips turn even the sweetest smile into a visual seduction. Thinking of her beauty in these terms always brings with it a flush of embarrassment and streak of anger. I'm not a poet or one of those sensitive guys that wears his heart on his sleeve and loves to share all his emotions in deep, meaningful conversations. I think that's all a bunch of useless bullshit.

I'm more comfortable when I admit she has the most slamming hot body on the planet. With long tanned legs, a tiny little waist, and curves that beg to be touched, no one can be blamed for letting their gaze linger. Our last encounter had given me personal knowledge of those curves and I'm honest enough to admit I want her and I want her bad. But my desire is riddled with guilt.

I know I can't continue staring at her in silence. I already look ridiculous. "Hey, Kinleigh. Good to see you." I work hard to keep my voice steady.

"Is it?" she asks, with a tilt of her head. "You don't act like it's good to see me."

Sighing, I shove my hands into my pockets and run the toe of my motorcycle boot over the edge of a loose brick on Logan and Charli's patio. I give it my full attention as a form of self-preservation.

I need to tell Logan about this so they can get it fixed. It's dangerous since all our friends are multiplying like rabbits lately. One of those kids will probably get hurt...
"Kyle?"
Shit. I'm stalling and we both know it.

Lifting my gaze, I see her hands have found her hips and she's pressed her pink, glossy lips together, causing their fullness to thin slightly. Unexpectedly, I want to laugh. She thinks she is so tough, but she just looks adorable. Unfortunately, thinking she is adorable is more dangerous that thinking she is hot.

"Kyle... Will you just talk to me?"

"I did talk to you," I say, with more gruffness than intended. "I said it was good to see you." I take a breath. "I need to go find Charli. I'll see you later." Forcing myself to walk away, her stare follows me and singes me with a penetrating heat.

I should leave, not just the backyard, but this whole damn ridiculous party. I've always been good at survival and this is definitely a time to put those skills to work for me.

Entering the living room, I notice Ronan seated on the couch, shooting glances between my sorry ass and the door I just pulled closed behind me with too much force. He's obviously caught on that I'm avoiding his daughter. For about the millionth time, I wonder exactly how much he knows about last summer.

Charli, always adept at reading situations, waddles over and slips her arm through mine. "Kyle, let me show you the nursery. I don't think you've seen it yet." I allow her to lead me away, even though I couldn't care less about a baby's room.

While rubbing circular patterns over her round, protruding belly, she leads me down the hallway to the far end of her new house. "Our baby girl should be making her grand appearance next month. I can't wait but..."

"But?" I ask with surprise. Charli and Logan had some fertility issues that I carefully avoided learning more about. I don't need to know the details of that kind of shit. But I do know how much they want this baby.

"Well like I said, I can't wait... but I'll admit I'm worried too," she confesses. "What if we aren't ready?" Lines settle across her forehead... and I don't like it. I'll always be protective of Charli, my independent and strong-willed friend, the woman that has always believed in me.

"You're a planner Charli," I remind her with a chuckle. "I'd put good money on you having everything you need and then some."

"I suppose." Her laugh is light but still bears traces of nervousness. "It's scary, though. What if I'm not a good mom?"

"You..." I tweak the end of her nose. "Will be an awesome mom. If Liv has managed to keep Ben alive, and in relatively good health for almost eight months, I might add... *you* have no worries."

Her laughter is genuine but quickly stifled when her guilt

9

kicks in. Liv is her best friend after all. "Kyle! You shouldn't say things like that! Liv is a great mother. Ben might have been an unexpected surprise in her life and she might be a little... unconventional... but she and Zac are good parents."

"I know. Don't get your giant, prego-sized panties in a twist. I was just teasing," I assure her. It earns me a quick punch. "But... neither one of us will be surprised if Ben's first word is 'fuck,' will we?"

She doesn't even try to stop the laughter this time. "No, I'm sure that poor kid will spend half his life with a bar of soap in his mouth from repeating his mother." Pushing open the last door on the left side of the hallway and grinning, she says, "Ta-da! What do you think?"

I walk into the nursery and smile. Leave it to Charli to make a baby's room cool. The walls are silvery gray, the crib is black wrought iron and all the bedding is pure white. "I thought everyone paints the nursery pink when they are having a girl."

"Pink isn't my thing," she reminds me, unnecessarily. The room's color scheme doesn't surprise me at all. Charli is a 'grey T-shirt, faded jeans, and old, black Converse' kind of girl. Pink doesn't play a part in her life.

Unbidden, my thoughts wander in the direction of another woman I know, a woman that can't get enough pink and girly frills in her life. *Why does everything lead me back to her?*

"The nursery is great," I tell Charli and I mean it.

"So..." She leans against the doorframe and crosses her arms under her chest and over that extended belly. I want to laugh at her. Barely five foot, with a tiny frame hijacked by that kid growing inside her, she looks ridiculously unbalanced. I keep expecting her to fall forward any second.

"What? I can tell you want to say something so just spit it

out." I'm afraid I know exactly what's on her mind.

"Can we talk about Kinleigh?"

"There's nothing to talk about." I walk further into the room and lightly tap the mobile of glittery stars and moons that hang above the crib.

"Kyle, I know you. Try again."

Damn. Charli holds a special place in my heart, always will, but she needs to mind her own business. "Kinleigh is off limits and you know it. Ronan is my boss and my friend. He would hand me my ass if I told him I wanted his daughter."

She walks over to join me at the crib and I feel her arm snake around me and give a quick squeeze. "I think you underestimate him. He loves Kinleigh and wants what's best for her... and he's smart enough to realize that could be you."

Sighing, I lean forward and rest my hands on the top rail of the crib. "Ronan and I are cool. I love working at his bar and I'm good at it... but he and I both know Kinleigh can do a lot better than some high school dropout bartender."

"Kyle!" Charli slaps my arm, probably thinking the hit was hard, but I barely felt it. I want to laugh when she points her index finger in my direction and starts to lecture. "You aced the equivalency test and then worked full time while getting your business degree. You don't just bartend at The Crash, you practically run the place now. You're smart and dedicated and loyal and anyone would be lucky to have you in their life."

"Damn. I forgot how funny you look when you're pissed," I tease, earning me another slap.

"Listen to me, Kyle Taylor... there is nothing you don't deserve! Understand?"

"Okay, okay... You sound like a mom already, Charli."

Her face relaxes into a smile and she takes a deep breath.

"What happened when Kinleigh was here last summer? It was obvious to anyone with eyes she was into you and I really thought you liked her too."

Unable to look her in the face, I study the stitched swirls on the baby's quilt. "Nothing happened. She's hot, end of story. I'll enjoy the scenery, but I'm not messing with the boss's daughter. No big deal. She isn't my type anyway."

"Not your type?" Charli asks with an incredulous grunt from the back of her throat. "Beautiful, smart and sweet isn't your type?"

"You know what I mean. The girl dresses like a fucking Barbie. She belongs at the country club, on the arm of a Ken doll. Her favorite thing to do is bake cupcakes, for God's sake. She is hearts and rainbows and will end up married to some suit, living in the suburbs with two kids and a dog."

"Kyle..." she starts.

"No, Charli. This discussion is over. Kinleigh isn't the woman for me and we both know it." I lean down and give her a quick peck on the top of her head. I'm done talking about things that will never be.

Chapter Two: Kinleigh

Cupcakes Are Better Than Sex

If Kyle thinks this is over, he is sadly mistaken!

Needing a few minutes to myself, I make an excuse to check on the dessert table. Besides, the cupcakes I brought might need restocking. Charli's dining room, situated near the front entrance, is barely large enough to accommodate the furniture, but it's an inviting mix of traditional charm and modern finishes and I like it. On the farthest wall is an antique dresser that doubles as a sideboard. That's where I find a tray of barely touched brownies that are a strange grey-brown color and topped with melted M&M's, a platter with dozens of sugar cookies displaying overly-browned edges, and my wrought iron cupcake stand... already half empty.

Earlier I'd stashed my plastic travel container with the extra cupcakes under the table, so I pull it out and carefully remove the remaining ones to refill the stand. Still not ready to join the other, my hands find busy work adjusting the table runner and scooping away crumbs as my mind wanders back to Kyle, as it usually does.

I know how people see me. I'm the one with the girlie clothes and a sweet smile – I must be a pushover... but they're wrong. Looking like my mom hides the core of steel I'd inherited from my dad. Kyle is about to learn he shouldn't underestimate me.

Lost in my own thoughts, I startle when I realize Liv has wandered in and is waiting for me to realize it. She kindly ignores my flustered delay and jumps right into conversation.

"I handed Ben off to his daddy and I'm hiding out for a minute to catch my breath," she explains. "I love my kid more than life itself, but he's like a tornado and I'm fucking exhausted!" I think I'm finally getting used to Liv's casual profanity and actually manage a quick laugh without the usual blush. It's hard when my mother raised me to believe that foul words were a sign you weren't smart enough to think of something worthwhile to contribute to the conversation. She also regularly threatened to tan my backside if she caught me embarrassing her in public with unladylike manners. Being raised in the south had definitely impacted Mom's ideas on child-rearing and I have to wonder what she'd make of my new friendship with Liv.

Unaware of my musings, Liv drops into the dining chair closest to the dessert table. Reaching an arm out to snag a chocolate and salted caramel cupcake, she runs the tip of her finger across the icing. She then pops the finger into her mouth and closes her eyes. Once her approval has been secured, a huge bite of the cupcake is followed by a wide smile and another bite. I love to see people enjoying the things I cook up in my kitchen.

Liv isn't urban-comfy like Charli. She isn't cutesy-sweet like everyone wants to label me. With her creamy skin, brilliant red hair and amazing hourglass figure... she is classically stunning and super edgy. Her distinctive style is a mix of modern sexy and vintage pinup. She always seems bigger than life and I admire her boldness that extends into every part of her life.

Finishing off the last crumb of her cupcake, she sighs with pleasure. "Oh my God... Kinleigh, these cupcakes are better than sex!"

"Hey!"

We both turn to see Zac striding into the room with an exaggerated frown on his face and their squirming son on his hip. He grins before making it to our side of the room, though. Considering he and Liv are about to be married, it's good he's not bothered by her frequent outbursts of sometimes inappropriate humor. There's no doubt Zac is crazy about her.

"Sorry... I should have said the cupcakes are *as good as* sex instead of *better*," Liv amends with a wink in my direction before lifting a cupcake up for him to taste. He takes a bite and his eyes widen.

"Damn. They *are* better than sex!" he agrees, resulting in him being the recipient of a quick punch to the arm from his fiancé.

I laugh. "Thanks."

"Num-num!" Ben yells out while lunging to steal the cupcake away from his father. Zac's quick reflexes save the poor baby from plummeting to the floor.

"Okay, okay!" Zac laughs, without skipping a beat at the near accident with his son, as he puts a smear of the icing into the baby's mouth.

"Zac! That's not good for him!" Liv yells while jumping up to save Ben from his dad's indulgence.

Ben doesn't want any part of Mommy while Daddy is holding the goods though and leans back as far away from her as he can.

Zac just continues to laugh and plays keep away, to Ben's delight. "He'll be fine, babe."

"I give up!" Liv shakes her head in defeat and falls back into her chair. "He likes you better anyway."

"Not when it's time for him to eat. Then it's all you." Zac throws her a wink and cocks a finger in her direction.

Liv just groans and closes her eyes. "Great. I'm his favorite because I have the boobs."

"Well, can you blame him?" Zac looks pointedly at Liv's chest and waggles his eyebrows ridiculously. "I rather like them too. In fact, I can't wait to..."

"Don't you dare say it, Zachary James Reynolds! Or Ben will be the *only one* enjoying these boobs for a while!"

Zac closes his mouths and mimes pulling a zipper across his lips before remembering I'm still here and addressing me. "You really did a fantastic job on the cupcakes, Kinleigh."

"Thanks. I didn't want to come to the housewarming party empty-handed, so I made them this morning. My dad's kitchen isn't ideal for baking but I managed to do okay, I hope. When I decided to move here, I loaded up my own gear and utensils from home, but I haven't had a chance to unpack all the boxes yet. Once I really settle in, be prepared for lots of treats!"

"So, you really are moving in with Ronan? I mean... I get that he's your dad and probably insisted but..." Liv's surprise is evident.

"I've finished college, but I don't have any real experience yet. Without that, my earning potential is a little dismal right now. Helping my dad out at the bar for a while seems like the best option and I can live with him rent free." I'm trying to put a positive spin on my decisions, but even I can hear how they sound like justifications. "Plus, my mom is pretty worried about me moving to the city and it is easier for her, knowing I'm staying with Dad. There aren't a lot of opportunities in my hometown."

Liv's eyes narrow and the corner of her mouth turns up slightly. She's smart and probably figures spending time around Kyle was also a deciding factor. She'd be right.

"Well as long as you keep the cupcakes coming our way, we hope you stay forever!" Zac says with a huge smile before reaching behind me and grabbing another cupcake for himself and possibly Ben.

"Thanks," I tell him. "I think?"

Liv dismisses Zac with a quick wave of her hand. "Don't listen to him. I think it will be good for Ronan to have you here. I'm just thinking about you staying at his place... His house is..."

"I know! It's awful!" I admit with a shudder. "All that dark paneling and heavy furniture and there's almost nothing on the walls. It's depressing. And he won't let me change a thing, of course."

"Have you considered getting your own place?" Zac asks while practically inhaling the dark chocolate cake and holding Ben as far away as he can. I watch the baby's chubby little legs kick in protest.

"I'd love to! I'm almost twenty-two now, but both of my parents seem to think I'm not ready to live on my own in the city. And I told you, with my 'just starting out income' I can't afford an apartment anywhere nice and that would double my mom and dad's anxiety. I don't want them to worry." I love my dad, but I'd be lying if I said spending the next six months or so in a house that is the dark lair of a confirmed bachelor won't be torture.

Zac licks the last of the crumbs from his fingers and sneaks a quick glance toward the sideboard and the remaining cupcakes. "What about the bar's apartment?" he suggests off-handedly while giving in and reaching for yet another. I'm amazed his trim body can consume so much. He's really tall, but that doesn't accommodate the number of cupcakes he's managed in just the last few minutes. He must have an awesome metabolism.

"It's no wonder our son eats like he does! How do you not have diabetes or something?" Liv complains, probably echoing my thoughts.

"Hey! It takes a lot of calories to fuel all this awesomeness," he assures her.

Liv rolls her eyes. "Even though you are eating cupcakes like you're fucking starving to death... your brain is apparently still fully functional. It's a good idea, Zac." Liv turns to me. "What do you think, Kinleigh?"

Their idea confuses me. Dad's bar has an amazing loft style apartment above it, but that's Liv's place. She and Charli had shared it in the beginning. When Charli married Logan and moved out, Liv had stayed. She and Ben are living there now. Is she asking me to be her new roommate? I think she's great, but could I actually live with her? Not to be mean, but she's messy and loud and... well... messy. "That's your home, Liv."

"I'm never there anymore. Ben and I are at Zac's place now with our wedding so close and I've been meaning to pack up all my shit and move it anyway. The apartment is great and your dad barely charges anything for rent. He is almost always at his bar downstairs... so he would feel like he's able to keep an eye on you but it would mean you don't have to actually live in his depressing man-cave of a house."

I feel a grin spread across my face as I clap my hands together in joy. "That would be perfect! Oh my God!" I think of the open, airy apartment and feel like dancing. "Thank you, so much!"

"Don't thank me. I didn't do anything and honestly, Ronan

18

may kill me for coming up with a plan to get you out from underneath his constant surveillance but... What can I say? I love that apartment and can't stand the thought of anyone undeserving getting it."

I jump up and down a little and wrap my arms around the curvy little redhead and squeeze while squealing near her ear.

"Ugh! Stop before I change my mind!" she says with a playful push to get me out of her personal space. I can tell she is pleased with the plan, though.

I close my eyes and try imagining how the space will look without all of Liv's clutter and the baby toys everywhere. The huge wall of windows keeps the apartment bright almost all the time. It's the exact opposite of my dad's dark, dreary house. My mind starts making lists of all the things I need to get started on. First up will be an oversized work island in that kitchen and convincing Daddy that installing an oven is essential for not just me but also future rentals. *How can anyone live without an oven?* Charli and Liv had survived with a microwave, but that's not normal. I already know the apartment will be perfect. It has all the room and privacy I need, it's right above the bar for work, and I'll be close enough to Kyle to convince him we belong together. Perfect.

Chapter Three: Kyle
Come Out, Come Out, Wherver You Are...

I am fucking ridiculous. I need to grow a pair and quit hiding in the damn pantry!

Just as I've finally convinced myself, it's time to man up and rejoin the party, the door to the large, walk-in pantry opens and the bright light of the kitchen shows me a silhouette I instantly recognize.

"What are you doing in here?" Kinleigh demands with a raised eyebrow and knowing smirk.

"Uh...I was looking for the extra paper towels. Charli said Ben spilled his drink and I... Ummm...I just..."

We both know it's a lie.

"You were looking for paper towels in the dark?" she asks with a small laugh.

Shit. Can't she just let me off the hook and leave? "What are you doing here?" I throw back in order to avoid answering her question.

"Wondering why you snuck off."

Shit.

"I didn't sneak off," I insist feebly.

"Uh huh," she laughs again and I feel a familiar tightening run through my body. She does this to me. When she's around it feels like the oxygen is being sucked out of the room and the badass cool I usually cultivate totally deserts me. I know I need to stay away from her, but it's so damn hard.

"What do you want, Kinleigh?" I groan.

"You, Kyle. I want you." She steps all the way into the pantry and closes the door behind her.

Standing together in the darkness, unable to see her, my other senses kick into overdrive. I smell her sugary sweetness that must have become part of her from the hours she spends baking. I can feel the warmth of her body only a few inches away from mine. I hear the soft pattern of her breathing increasing in rhythm with every second. I want her more than I've ever wanted anything.

"Kinleigh... This is a bad idea," I whisper in desperation.

"No, Kyle, this is a very, very good idea." She closes the little bit of distance remaining between us and wraps her arms around me.

Without my brain's consent, my hands bury themselves in her long, silky hair and she sighs. Her delicate fingers run over my back and shoulders and eventually land on either side of my face. She increases the pressure of her grasp and pulls my head down to her. Trying to resist her is impossible. I give in and sink into the pleasure of her kiss. Her soft lips and exploring tongue are enough to make me forget every good excuse I'd concocted to stay away from her.

Pushing her back against the pantry shelves, I slide my thigh between her legs and nudge them apart. I bite gently on her bottom lip and she laughs before reaching around and slipping her hands into the back pockets of my jeans and pulling me in tighter. I groan and throw my right arm out to grasp the edge of the shelf behind her, hoping for support, and knock several canned goods down. A few roll away, but one must have landed on Kinleigh's foot.

"Owww!" she yells, jerking back away from me.

Then we both hear a voice coming into the kitchen and go silent. "I swear she came in here, Liv," Ronan says, and the sound of his heavy boots on the tiled floor say he's coming closer.

"Uh...no. I don't think so. Did you check the nursery? Charli has been making everyone check it out like it's the first room ever decorated for a child in the history of mankind," Liv answers hurriedly.

"She isn't in the nursery. She came into the kitchen," Ronan insists.

Liv's voice is now very close and a thud against the pantry's door convinces me she must be leaning on it. "Well, she isn't here now! Go check the backyard. She's probably playing with all the kids."

There's an aggravated grunt from Ronan. "I don't suppose you know where Kyle is right now? You don't think it's a little strange they've both disappeared?"

"Kyle? Oh... I think he's in the bathroom."

"We just passed the bathroom, Liv. No one was in it," he reminds her.

"He went to the master bathroom. He probably had to shit and didn't want to do it in the guest one."

I feel Kinleigh's body shaking with laughter. *I'm going to kill*

Liv.

"Something isn't right about this," Ronan says, but his receding footsteps relax me enough to resume breathing.

Liv raps her hand lightly on the door. "Okay, you two can come out now. Your dad is gone, Kinleigh."

Opening the door a crack, we lean close and peer out. As promised, Ronan is gone. We walk out of the pantry to find Liv leaning on the kitchen island, smiling from ear to ear. "You know I played a lot of ten minutes in the closet in my teen years. Half an hour in the pantry while in your twenties seems a little unnecessary. You're old enough to mess around somewhere more private now. Don't you have an apartment, Kyle?"

"Shut up, Liv," I tell her.

"You can even get busy at my apartment if you need it. I'll be at Zac's tonight," Liv responds.

"Shut up, Liv," I tell her again.

Threading her arm through mine, Kinleigh turns to face Liv with a big smile. I notice her pink lip gloss is smeared onto her chin and I want to reach up with my thumb and gently swipe it away, but that would seem too personal and possessive. I don't want her and Liv getting the wrong idea about what Kinleigh is to me.

"Thank you, Liv," Kinleigh says with a big grin and tilt of her head. "That was really nice of you to divert Dad so he didn't find us. This isn't how I wanted to tell him about Kyle and me."

I pull away from Kinleigh, close my eyes and count to ten. *Hadn't I learned my lesson last time? She just doesn't get it!* "There's nothing to tell him, Kinleigh."

"What do you mean?" she asks through clenched teeth. One hand is on her hip and the other is tapping the granite countertop closest to her.

"Okay... I'm out!" Liv says, throwing her hands up in defeat. "Catch you later." It takes Liv less than two seconds to vacate the kitchen.

Kinleigh stops the finger-tapping in order to cross her arms and glare at me. Her lips are in a tight pucker and her eyes are narrowed, but she is still adorable. I catch myself fixating on the smudge of lip gloss, fighting the urge to touch it.

"Kinleigh...I..." *Fuck. What the hell can I say that I didn't already say last summer?*

"Are we still singing this song?" she asks. "My big, bad Daddy won't approve? I'm too young for you? I deserve someone better than you? Blah, blah, blah... Try a new tune, Kyle. I've heard it all and I'm not impressed. This is my life, not my dad's, and I get to choose the people in it. You are seven years older than me, but we're both adults and it doesn't matter. You have a steady job, a newly acquired college degree, and despite trying to act like you are so tough...you are one of the kindest and most generous men I've ever met. So quit whining and pushing me away!"

Walking over to her, I stand close enough to touch. I can actually feel the warmth of her desire and anger and grit my teeth to hold back from closing that last final inch between us. Wanting her, always wanting her... but knowing it's better this way, I pull my mouth into the familiar smirk I've perfected to hide what I don't want people to see. Men read it as cocky and condescending. Women usually take it as a challenge and try even harder. But I know Kinleigh. It will piss her off.

Now it's time for the final touch. Licking my thumb, I finally wipe the lip gloss from her chin and watch her quick intake of breath.

"I'm not pushing you away, babe. I'll leave with you right now if that's what you really want," I whisper as I run my nose up the side of her cheek and breathe into her ear.

"You will?" she whispers back. She wants to believe me. She wants to believe we are finally on the same page, but my expression is enough to create a ripple of skepticism.

"Abso-fucking-lutely. We can go back to my place." I run my hand lightly down her arm. "We can do every naughty little thing you ever dreamed about and some you've never even imagined."

"Oh..." I watch her pupils dilate as she swallows hard and her chest begins to rise and fall even faster.

"We will have lots of fun." She melts a little more. "But... if your dad finds out you decided to be one of my girls he will fire my ass. I happen to like my job. So you keep those pretty little lips sealed." I place one finger over her lips to emphasize my point. "Got it, Princess?"

I see when my words fully register. She jerks away from me in disgust.

"One of your girls, Kyle?" she hisses.

"Sure... if that's what you want, Kinleigh," I tell her. "I only accept willing participants."

She pulls away and turns her back to me. "Why are you doing this?" Every line of her posture betrays her pain.

I want to take it all back. I want to apologize and beg forgiveness. I'm a complete asshole for trying to make her feel cheap and expendable, but I know it's for the best. I'm going to see this through. One of us has to put an end to the ridiculous dream she has of us ever being something more to each other.

"Doing what? I'm just giving you what you obviously want. We've messed around a few times but no more playing, Kinleigh. Let's do this thing and get it out of our system so we can move on."

Slowly, she turns back to me. "Playing?"

"I get it, okay? The spoiled princess that wants a hot night with the bad boy her parents wouldn't approve of. Fine. I'll be your little fantasy and enjoy the benefits of getting a piece of that fine ass."

She's fast. I don't see the slap coming but I sure as hell feel it.

"You are an asshole, Kyle Taylor." The low calm of her voice is worse than if she'd yelled.

"Yes, I am," I whisper to the now empty room.

Chapter Four: Kinleigh
Hope

I lean past him and take control of the mouse, navigating back to his account overview page. "Dad, this would be so much easier if you let me update your software. I could just..."

"There's nothing wrong with the way I do things here, Kinleigh." He steals the mouse back and turns his shoulder to block me from regaining access to his ancient computer.

"I didn't say you were wrong." I hop on to the corner of his desk and cross my arms. "I said there is an *easier* way."

My father crosses his arms right back at me and gives me *the* glare. It might intimidate everyone else but not me. I understand him. Set in his ways, he hates to admit he doesn't have every situation under control. Eventually, I'll convince him to see my side of it.

"Easy isn't always best." He leans back in his chair and points a thick finger in my direction. That's what is wrong with your generation." He winds up for a nice long lecture I'm not in the mood to hear.

Smiling sweetly, I slide off the desk and bend down to give him a squeeze. He relaxes. He loves me. "I know, Daddy. The gosh darn whippersnappers in this decade are lazy. They think the world owes them something. What's wrong with good, old-fashioned hard work?"

"Are you being sassy with me?"

"I just feel like it's time for you to stand out in your yard and yell for the neighborhood kids to get off your lawn!"

He hides a laugh with an irritable grunt. "Just finish the accounts, Kinleigh and keep your mouth closed. I get enough of that crap from my waitresses. Against my better judgment, I gave in to your demand for the upstairs apartment. I gave you a job at my bar to help you get some work experience. Can you just give me a break for once?" Giving me a quick hug to soften his words, he gets up and leaves me alone in the office.

Still grinning, I slide into the desk chair, careful to avoid setting my arms down on the cracked leather armrests that pinch with a vengeance, and pull the keyboard of the crappy desktop computer closer.

The Crash is a great bar. It's modern and hip, has a great location in the heart of the city's upscale business district, and even showcases popular, local bands regularly. My dad has a lot to be proud of. His office is another story. Calling it shabby is polite. The walls are a sickly green, the furniture has seen better days, and the only decoration is a perpetual calendar with fighter jets across the top and an old metal sign promising cold bottles of RC Cola for a nickel.

I run my pearly pink fingernail down the monitor and check the numbers against the inventory print out beside me. The bar's books are accurate, but I need to make my dad understand he is making this harder and much more time consuming than it should be. His system could be so much more efficient if...

"Hey."

My head jerks up at the sound of his voice. Avoiding Kyle at work since the horrible scene at Charli's housewarming party has been my top priority and so far I've done pretty well. I stick to the office mostly and when I venture out into the bar, I stick close to Madison, the waitress I'm fast becoming friends with.

"What can I help you with?" I look back at the computer and avoid his gaze.

There's no need to look at him anyway. I have him memorized. Dark, thick hair falls right below his wide shoulders and his eyes are edged in espresso, only lightening slightly to a warm chocolate near the pupils. And why do guys always end up with those long, thick lashes but women have to wear extensions and mascara to achieve the same effect? His muscles are well-defined and highlighted perfectly by the impressive collection of tattoos that show from beneath the sleeves of his T-shirt. I've even seen the one that runs across his shoulder blades and down his spine. He's a work of art. But besides all the physically attractive attributes this man was graced with, there is something more. He has something indefinable and irresistible that holds a promise worthy of any sin you need to commit. No matter what awful thing he does, I still seem to want him.

He still hasn't said a word, so I give in and look up. "Kyle? Do you need something?"

He clears his throat. "I need a copy of the last order to our beer distributor. The delivery is here and it doesn't look right to me. I know we asked for more cases of Shiner." His voice is calm and efficient. It betrays none of the chaos I'm experiencing.

Here stands the man that can set my body on fire with a single touch or completely break my heart with a few cruel words.

I stand up and grab a folder from the file cabinet to the left of the desk. "Okay, got it." Walking briskly, I almost make it past him and through the door when he grabs my arm. His grip is soft but firm and even though I'm still so pissed right now I could cry in frustration, by body betrays me. My pulse quickens and there is an electric tingle radiating across my skin, causing me to shiver slightly.

Kyle plucks the folder out of my hand. "I can take care of it," he whispers too close to my ear. I can actually feel the warmth of his breath on the side of my face.

I will *not* let him know what he is doing to me. Grabbing the folder back from him, I smile. "Thanks anyway but this is what I'm being paid for."

Kyle laughs. "I was just trying to help, Princess."

"I don't need your help. I don't need anything from you." His hand is still wrapped around my upper arm, making it impossible for me to leave the small office.

"We all have needs." Kyle steps even closer. Placing a finger under my chin, he lifts my face so that I see his dark, mischievous eyes staring right at me. I'm caught. I can't move. "And right now I have a need."

I swallow hard. Taking a deep breath and holding it, I wait for his next words.

"I *need* this folder so I can check our beer order," he says, pivoting quickly and leaving me alone. It takes several seconds for me to realize I'm no longer in possession of the folder. He had managed to snatch it from me without me even realizing it. *Asshole.*

Taking a few much-needed gulps of air, I grab my purse off

the hook by the door and rummage around for my small mirror. My cheeks are flushed and my lip gloss is almost non-existent. Basically, I look a mess and I can't stand strong and do what needs to be done when I don't look my best. Repairing my makeup, I firm my resolve and straighten my spine. It is time to put on my big girl panties and do my job.

Marching into the storage room, I manage to slip past Kyle quickly and slide myself right next to the delivery guy. He's young, probably close to my age, and not bad looking. I flash him a big smile and tilt my head.

"Hi," I say. "I'm Kinleigh and I'm in charge of deliveries now. Catch me up on the problem."

"Oh...Hi!" the delivery guy answers, turning to face me and completely ignoring the pissed off Kyle. "I'm Pete. I'm new to this route. I deliver beer. It's a new job, but I like it. You know, I deliver beer and I like it a lot. A whole lot."

Pete's eyes are running up and down my body with only brief stops on my face. He can't quit smiling. I'm a smart woman and I expect to be respected for my business knowledge. I don't want to use my appearance to further my career or get my way... but the look on Kyle's face is making it hard for me to resist. A little flirting with this stammering young man is very tempting since it would probably remind Kyle that two can play his game.

Poor Pete. It's not his fault I'm hot for the bartender and trying to make him jealous. As tempting as it is, though... I just can't lead the delivery guy on for my own personal gain.

Stepping back a little, I smile pleasantly but keep my stance firm and refuse to put a hand on my hip like I normally would. "It is very nice to meet you, Pete. Can I see today's invoice for comparison? I'm sure this can be cleared up easily."

Hearing the heavy stomps of Kyle's boots retreating behind

31

me, I turn just as he slams the storage room's door closed, leaving me alone with Pete. *What did Kyle expect? Did he really think he could bulldoze me out of the way and treat me like my father's charity case instead of a real employee?*

Carefully fending off Pete's hints about us going out sometime, I manage to clear up the discrepancy and send him on his way after about ten or fifteen minutes. Proud of myself, I go into the bar to look for Kyle. He's behind the counter, lining up all the liquor bottles and prepping for tonight's shift.

"We figured it out," I tell him. "Pete will make another stop tomorrow to drop off the missing cases."

Kyle lets go of the thick-bodied bottle of Crown and turns to face me. Resting his arms on the bar in front of him, I can see the tension making his muscles pop more noticeably through the thin sleeves of his faded T-shirt.

"I'm sure you and *Pete* have it all figured out, Kinleigh." His voice could cut glass and I flinch.

"What is that supposed to mean?" I hiss as I come around the bar to stand right next to him.

He smirks. "You had that poor kid wrapped around your little finger, Princess. He would probably deliver a whole fucking truckload of beer at no charge if you flashed him another couple inches of your..."

"You've lost your mind!" I interrupt and give him a quick shove in the center of his chest. "I'm just doing my job." I give him another shove. "You are just jealous that I was able to figure out the problem so quickly without you!" I attempt yet another shove but before I can push, Kyle grabs my wrists and holds both of my hands over his heart.

"You're right. I was jealous." His voice is soft and his expression is softer.

All heat from my anger drains away and I'm stunned into silence. This is the Kyle I remember. This is the Kyle from last summer that made me want to pack up all my belongings and move in with my dad to be closer to him. His more recent behavior still hurts and I know I shouldn't give him another opportunity to tear at my heart.

"I have things to do," Kyle whispers, unable to look at me any longer. He releases my hands and leaves me alone... but with a hope that makes me feel foolish.

Chapter Five: Kyle
Dp You Want My Cupcake?

I have a plan. I'll knock on her door, tell her that Ronan needs her to come down to the bar an hour early today... and then get my ass gone before I forget that it's best for me to stay away from her.

Piece of cake.

My fist is just about to make contact with her apartment door when I stop. From inside I can hear muffled but very loud... singing? I lower my hand and lean my ear closer. *Yeah...definitely singing.*

"Baby, Baby, Baby, oooohhhh..."

I can't help it. I start to laugh. *Justin Bieber?* I let my head fall forward and my forehead thunks against the door harder than I meant. The singing stops and a few seconds later the door opens.

"Kyle!"

I should deliver the message and run. Instead, I stand there with an idiot grin on my face, checking her out from head to toe.

Her pale blonde hair is in a wild mess held in place by a hot pink clip with its teeth sunk deeply into the strands. She has on a thin white tank top, providing only minimal coverage of her neon pink bra. I assume her too-long flannel pants, also hot pink with large white polka-dots, are pajamas because when my gaze finally comes to rest at their hem, all I can see are fluffy white bunnies with pink noses where her feet should be.

"What are you doing here?" she asks. Her slightly accusatory tone sends a twinge of regret through my heart. She has every right to question my motives. I'm questioning them right now myself.

Reaching up with my thumb, I wipe a smear from her cheek and ignore her question. "Is this icing?"

Kinleigh turns around self-consciously and begins scrubbing at her face with a small kitchen towel. "Yeah, I was attempting a new flavor for my dad." She turns back to face me and smiles. I can't help it, I smile back.

"What flavor?" I ask with real curiosity. She's been trying for weeks to get Ronan to sell her cupcakes along with the drinks. He's told her no in every way imaginable, but she refuses to give up. Obviously, 'the stubborn gene' runs rampant in that family.

Grabbing my arm, she pulls me into the apartment and drags me over to the kitchen space. On a portable kitchen island, there are several mixing bowls, a huge pink mixer, pink spatulas, a bottle of bourbon, and a plate of bacon.

"You are making bacon bourbon cupcakes?" It doesn't surprise me. I think she can make anything into a cupcake.

Grinning, she claps her hands together and bounces lightly. "Okay, so I made a bourbon infused cupcake with a maple bacon frosting. Want to try it?"

My God, she's the sexiest thing ever. "You had me at bourbon, babe."

She dips her finger into the mixing bowl and extracts a glob of caramel-colored frosting. When she reaches toward my mouth, my brain screams for me to retreat but other parts of my body insist I lean closer and suck her finger into my mouth.

Brains are highly overrated.

The frosting is delicious but even when every trace of it is gone, I continue to gently suck and lick the tip of her finger. Instead of pulling away, she tilts her head back and closes her eyes. I grab her forearm and place gentle kisses on her palm and the underside of her wrist.

"I'm pretty messy when I bake," she confides in a whisper, "but I don't think I got icing there."

"I just thought I should be thorough. You never know." I run my tongue from her wrist, up the underside to the bend of her arm while holding her elbow.

She giggles, huskily. "Thanks, Kyle. How very thoughtful of you."

Letting go of her, I wrap one arm around her waist and use my other to clasp her hand in mine. I slowly begin swaying. "You know what we really need right now?" I ask her.

"What?" she breathes into my ear.

"Music."

"Oh...okay. I have my iPod speaker on the counter and I could..."

I interrupt her. "Oh, Kinleigh... we don't need your iPod."

Looking up in confusion, she asks, "we don't?"

"Nope. You could just sing me some of that Bieber-Fever you were belting out when I came upstairs." I can't hold it in any longer. My escaped laughter makes our dancing impossible.

She slaps my arm and huffs, but she's laughing too. "So is it more embarrassing that I got caught singing the Biebs... or that you recognized the song?"

"Point taken," I respond, good-naturedly.

She grabs one of the unfrosted cupcakes from a cooling rack near the sink and waggles it in front of my face. "You tried the frosting... Do you want to try my cupcake?"

I groan, unable to resist her any longer. "More than you know."

She steps closer. "It's yours for the taking."

Ignoring the cupcake in her hand, I grab hold of her waist and lift her up onto the only small section of counter that isn't covered in baking paraphernalia. She opens her knees to let me in closer and I feel her hook her legs around my back. In the back of my mind, I'm aware that this action means I have two fluffy white bunnies tangled behind me and it must look ridiculous.

I don't give a shit.

Finally dropping the cupcake, she runs her long pink fingernails into my hair and the sensation of them lightly clawing across my scalp is heaven. I run quick kisses down her neck and collarbone and she moans softly. Then she takes a firm hold of my hair and forces my face up to her. I get the hint.

Our lips come together hard and this kiss releases all the frustration and agony of trying to stay away from her. I want her more than I've ever wanted anyone or anything in my life. I cannot get enough of her.

My hands travel down to grasp the edge of her tank top and we break apart just long enough for me to pull it upward. It gets caught momentarily but she yanks the clip holding her hair and it releases the shirt with it.

The neon pink of her sports bra is almost blinding. *Where in the hell does she find clothing in this color? It looks like it should be a highlighter!*

I reach for the small metal hooks on the front of the bra, happy for the convenience they provide. I have the topmost hook undone when she closes her hands over mine and stops them.

"Let me," she whispers and I nod.

Hell yeah.

We had messed around some when she was here last summer and I'd even had the privilege of holding those phenomenal breasts in my hands, but it had been in the back of the storage room and very dark. The idea of finally seeing their perfection has me unable to breathe properly. I feel like I'm back in junior high, about to see boobs for the first time after asking Carrie Miller to be my girlfriend.

Kinleigh deftly unhooks the second closure and I take a deep breath. Two more until those babies are released for my viewing pleasure. I hear the little snap as the third releases... and then I hear something else. Something that wrecks my dreams.

"Kinleigh? Kyle?" Ronan's deep voice booms up the staircase from the bar below and is followed by the heavy stomp of his boots ascending.

"Oh, crap..." Kinleigh groans while unhooking her legs from me and jumping down from the counter. With lightning speed, she snaps the bra back up and scrambles for the discarded tank top. I see it first and help her pull it over her head. Her hair looks like she just came in from a windstorm but there's not time to fix it. Ronan is turning the knob and the kitchen is entirely visible from the door.

Kinleigh shoves a cupcake into my hand and turns to face her father. "Hi, Daddy!" she says a little too brightly.

Ronan looks from her crazy hair to my guilty face. "What's

going on?" he asks.

Kinleigh grabs another cupcake, spoons a quick smear of the frosting onto it and pushes it toward Ronan. "I asked Kyle to stay a minute and try my new cupcakes. Here..." She puts the cupcake into Ronan's reluctant hand. "Try it. I really think you should sell these in the bar, Daddy. Kyle said they're good. It has bourbon and bacon! Try it!"

Her machine gun fire of conversation, flushed face, and nervous smile make Ronan frown even harder. He isn't stupid.

"Kyle..." Ronan turns to me.

"Yeah."

"I think you've had enough cupcakes for today. You need to get back to the bar...now."

I look over at Kinleigh and she mouths, "sorry."

"I'm gone," I say and leave the apartment. It is obvious that Ronan feels the same as I do about this. I'm not good enough for Kinleigh.

Chapter Six: Kinleigh
Pick Your Poison

"You know you don't have to be down here in the bar during operating hours. The office work can be handled during the day," my dad tells me...again. He's normally out front, overseeing everything during the shifts but when he needed something from his office, he had asked me to join him.

"I like helping out, Dad. Besides, living above the bar means I'm not going to bed early. The noise drifts up."

"That's why you should have stayed at my house! It's nice and quiet there. You don't need to be out hanging out in a bar every night!"

I walk over and rest my head on his shoulder. "It's not just a bar. It's your bar and my job. I'm not drinking or partying and I like to be useful. As for staying with you, we've discussed this many times. I love my apartment. And it was time for me to have my own place."

He scowls. "So you can bake cupcakes for Kyle?"

I scowl back. "Don't start! Kyle is a great guy. You should be happy I'm interested in him. You've told me for years what a good employee he is, what a level head he has and how you want good things for him. Why can't I be that good thing?"

"I meant he is a smart kid and has the potential to do well for himself. I didn't mean I was grooming him to take my daughter."

"No one is *taking* me. Can we please NOT discuss this again? You are a broken record!" I stare at him until looks away. He knows I can be just as hard-headed as him.

"I've got stuff to do," he growls and leaves the office, closing the door behind him with a loud bang. Refusing to stay put, I open the door back up and run right into a waitress walking toward the row of pool tables.

"Sorry!" I grab her elbow in time to save the empty glasses that fill her round tray. I'm happy to notice it's Madison.

"I'm fine," she assures me. "But, what did you do to piss your dad off?" she asks with round, fearful eyes. "He stomped off to the storage room like you'd told him you decided to work at the strip club two blocks over!"

I smile at her. Madison had filled in when Liv took a long photography assignment a couple of years ago. She performed so well, she became the permanent replacement when Liv gave birth to her son Ben and decided that being a Mommy and shooting an occasional photography assignment was all she could handle.

"Dad just doesn't like the idea of me dating Kyle," I tell her with a shrug. "He'll get over it."

Madison frowns at me. "You and Kyle?"

"Yeah, I know things have been tense between us lately but earlier this afternoon, before the shift started, he came up to my apartment and..." I blush. "Well, he was different. And he was willing to try, I could tell. I think everything is going to work out."

"He said that? He said that you two are together now?"

"Well... not officially or anything but..." I smile at her, but she doesn't smile back. She looks nervous. I watch her bite at her bottom lip and take a deep breath. "Madison? What's wrong?"

"It's just that... I mean Kyle is..." Her eyes dart over my shoulder, in the direction of the long bar that runs across the left side of the room.

Following her gaze, I turn to see Kyle leaned halfway across the bar, obviously flirting with a very attractive brunette in a red dress so tight I'm surprised she can breathe.

Madison pats my shoulder sympathetically. "Sorry, Kinleigh. Kyle is hot and I adore him... but he's kind of a player. I had a huge crush on him when I first started working here, but I was already in love with my boyfriend Mike, thankfully, so it saved me from getting my heart broken."

Kyle had tried to warn me that I could do better than him. My dad tried to tell me Kyle wasn't right for me. I hadn't listened. This is my fault.

"I think maybe I'm done for the night, Madison." I start to walk toward the back of the bar, to the door that will allow me to escape to my apartment. She reaches out to stop me.

"Wait, don't go." She looks over toward Kyle and then back to me. "Don't you know that the best thing you can do is stay and act like it doesn't bother you at all? As I said, I adore Kyle, but if he's been stringing you along then, you need to give him a taste of his own medicine."

I knew there was a reason I liked Madison. "What did you have in mind?" I ask.

"You've helped me out in the past enough to handle a table

or two of your own. Check out the two that just sat down at table six. A very cute blonde and a tall guy with reddish brown hair. Pick your poison."

I look over to check out the guys she mentioned. She's right. They are both very attractive. "You want me to wait on that table?"

"Why not? I have my man already and we shouldn't let this opportunity go to waste. Maybe a little...or a lot... of flirting will be just what you need right now," she tells me.

I smile. "Okay. I'll grab a tray."

Madison hands over her own with a flourish. "I'll get a new one. Go!"

Flipping my hair over my shoulder and straightening my posture, I flash a quick smile in Kyle's direction – he is watching me intently now – and head for table six.

"Welcome to The Crash. What can I get you?" I ask with my best smile and perky attitude.

The darker haired guy answers immediately. "Baby...I'm buying whatever you're selling!"

"Dude!" The blonde punches him lightly. "Not cool!" He looks up at me and smiles apologetically. "I'm sorry for my friend's bad manners. He regularly embarrasses me in public."

I laugh. "It's fine."

"No," he insists. "It's not. Just because you are the most beautiful woman, I think I've ever seen... it's not an excuse to be obnoxious."

"Damn, Jeremy! You don't have to make me sound like a douchebag," the friend complains.

The blonde ignores him and puts his hand out in my direction. "Hi. I'm Jeremy. And my occasionally rude friend is Ryan."

I shake his hand and smile again. "It's nice to meet you. I'm

Kinleigh."

"Believe me, Kinleigh... meeting you is the nicest thing that has happened to me in a long time," Jeremy says, reluctantly letting go of my hand.

"Thank you. I kind of needed to hear that right now."

He frowns. "Has someone upset you tonight? Point them out to me. I'll take care of it."

I laugh. "Thanks but it's under control. Truly. What can I get you to drink?"

The guys place their order and I walk to the bar with a shot of confidence running hot in my veins. Kyle is still staring at me and he never breaks eye contact from the moment I left the table to the time I make it to where he now stands.

"I need a rum and coke and a Heineken," I tell him.

Kyle doesn't budge. "Why are you waiting on Madison's table?"

"She asked me to help." I look over my shoulder and smile at Jeremy. He smiles back. "And I really don't mind."

"I don't like the way he's looking at you."

"Well, what you like or don't like has no influence over me, Kyle. We aren't dating...remember?" I look pointedly at the girl in the tight red dress, still seated near the bar, and then back at Kyle. He understands but scowls.

"No, we aren't," he says firmly.

"So you just fill that drink order and let me get back to Jeremy, okay?" I set my tray down on the bar top and he turns to make the drinks.

Little Miss Red-Dress takes that moment to call down the length of the bar. "Kyle? Could you please get me another?" She shakes her empty glass to emphasize her need.

Kyle gives her that sexy smirk he's perfected. "There's nothing I'd like more, Tammy. Well... maybe one or two things that I might like a little more are coming to mind." He winks in her direction and she giggles.

"You are an asshole, Kyle." I grab my drinks. "Have fun with Tammy." I turn and practically sprint back to Jeremy's table. Kyle is calling my name, but I ignore him.

"Here you go, gentlemen." I set the drinks down in front of them.

"Thanks," says Ryan.

"See... I taught him some manners while you were away," Jeremy says with a wink.

"And I thought chivalry was dead!" I respond.

The rest of the night goes smoothly. I help Madison with a few of her tables but spend most of my time avoiding Kyle and talking with Jeremy and Ryan. They're funny and Jeremy is particularly sweet and attentive. Right before closing, I bring them their tab.

"You can settle up with me or take this to the register at the end of the bar," I tell them.

"Oh, I'd much rather let you take care of it," Jeremy says with a flirty, crooked grin before handing me more than enough cash to cover the bill. "And I don't want the change. It's for you."

"Thanks," I respond, with an answering grin.

"Kinleigh?" I feel Jeremy tentatively take hold of my arm to stop me from leaving. "I don't want to be presumptuous but could I get your number?"

"My number?"

Do I want to give my phone number to this stranger? He's been so nice all evening, but I'm still hesitant. I know it's pathetic to be pining for Kyle when he doesn't want me but can I really go out with someone else?

I look over at Kyle and see him accepting a napkin from Tammy. He folds it up, puts it in the pocket of jeans and smiles at her.

Screw him. Why not?

"Sure, Jeremy. I'll give you my number. Hand me your phone." He does as I've asked and I program it in for him.

"Can I call you tomorrow? I'd love to take you out sometime." He and Ryan stand up and grab their jackets off the back of the chairs.

"That would be wonderful."

Jeremy's face breaks into a huge smile. "Great. Talk to you soon."

I wipe down the table after they leave and then take my tray behind the bar to stow it under the counter. I think Kyle has gone to the back and I try to hurry so I can avoid him. I'm almost successful... but not quite.

I have my hand on the door that leads to my apartment stairs when I can feel him behind me. I stand there, refusing to turn around or make a sound. Seconds tick by and then I feel him gently lifting the long strands of my hair and pushing them away from my neck. I stop breathing.

"Kinleigh..." he breathes right into my ear.

I've had enough. I can't take all the back and forth anymore. I jerk away from him and turn to glare. "What, Kyle?"

"Don't go out with that guy. I have a bad feeling about him."

I close my eyes and take a deep breath before answering. "Goodnight, Kyle." I go through the door, close it firmly behind me, and run up the steps like the hounds of hell are after me.

Chapter Seven: Kyle
An Unexpected Blessing

Last night had been brutal. The cupcake encounter in Kinleigh's apartment had convinced me to just give in and let her know what she means to me. Fuck the consequences. I'd tried for too long to do the right thing, but it was making me miserable. I didn't deserve another shot with her but by some miracle, she hadn't rejected me. She still seemed to want me. I was in heaven when I'd slid her onto her counter and gave in to my baser instincts.

And then Ronan had shown up and reminded me I belong in hell. He couldn't have been any clearer. I needed to get my worthless ass away from his daughter.

Using every diversion I could think of to avoid her hadn't worked long. Finally, I had resorted to the lowest tactic I could think of. Knowing Kinleigh was watching, I had shown interest in one of the women hanging at the bar. I don't remember her name or what she looked like, and it was a shitty move on my part to lead the woman on, but I'd run out of ideas.

My plan had worked. It also had unexpected consequences. The next guy that smiled and fed Kinleigh a line of bullshit got her attention. It had sent a blinding jealousy straight through me that I had no justification for. *What had I expected to happen?* This creep had the right clothes, the right haircut, and a smooth confidence. I hated him instantly.

I'm usually a good judge of character and I don't trust him. In all fairness, I know this could be the result of my jealousy but what if it's more? Does he deserve my wariness? I can't think of Kinleigh choosing to be with anyone that wouldn't cause me to secretly contemplate a little bodily harm. I shouldn't be with her but I don't want anyone else to have her. I'm the worst kind of asshole.

The bar isn't open yet and the quiet is giving me too much time to think. Even though she isn't here, I see Kinleigh everywhere. I remember the way she smiles at me over her shoulder every time she walks away. I love how she laughs and manages to tease me clear of any threat of bad temper. She's unfailing kind to everyone and always willing to help but strong enough to make sure she's never taken advantage of. And every time I look at her, I just...

"Kyle! Get in here!"

Ronan's voice is an effective executioner to my pointless daydreams. Closing the small refrigerator of juices kept under the bar, I turn reluctantly toward the office. His command is loud and clear. I don't consider myself chicken shit but I'm not brave enough to ignore him.

Leaning against the doorframe of his office, I'm hoping it will be quick. "What's up?" I ask with false bravado.

"Come in and close the door behind you." He's looking down at a stack of invoices on his desk as he motions me in.

Shit.

Doing as he asks, I sit in the folding metal chair opposite him. Seconds tick by with neither of us saying a word or even making eye contact. I feel myself starting to sweat. Ronan and I have always been cool in the past but since Kinleigh's arrival... it's been awkward. I'll admit to avoiding him when possible.

How in the hell do you look a guy in the face when all you want to do is get naked and nasty with his daughter?

I clear my throat, unable to take the silence anymore. "What's up?"

Ronan steeples his fingers and leans forward until his chin is resting on top of them. "I want to talk to you about Kinleigh."

Shit.

I lean back in the chair, trying to keep cool. "What about Kinleigh?"

"Look... I... uh..." He looks around the room, searching for inspiration. "I think you are an okay guy, Kyle."

"Okay... Thanks...I guess?"

"It's just that well... Kinleigh is my daughter and I..."

I stand up and the chair makes an awful protest as the metal legs scrape against the concrete floor. Recognizing where this is headed, I'll save us both some time. "I get it, Ronan. She deserves a lot better than me. I already know. I told her all of this, so spare me the lecture." Turning toward the door, hell bent on ending this nightmare as soon as possible, I throw a parting promise over my shoulder. "I won't mess with her. She is off limits. You don't have to..."

"Oh, shut the fuck up, Kyle!" The boom of his voice momentarily freezes me. It takes Ronan all of two seconds to reach my side and let his hand fall heavily upon my shoulder. When he steers me back to my chair, I let him. *What choice do I have?*

"How about you listen to me instead of assuming you know what I want to say?" Frustration adds another layer to his ever-present scowl.

"Okay. I'm sorry. I just thought that I should let you know that I agree with you and Kinleigh should..."

"Didn't I tell you to shut up?" The dangerous quiet of his tone does more to silence me than his yelling ever would. "As I was saying... Kyle, you aren't a bad guy. No one will ever be good enough for Kinleigh in my book but if she has to end up with someone... you aren't too bad of a someone."

Wait, what? Did Ronan just give me his blessing to date his daughter?

"Close your mouth. You look like an idiot," Ronan tells me.

"So... let me get this straight... you think I should go out with... Kinleigh? Kinleigh Walters? Your daughter?" This is making no sense at all.

"I didn't say I was going to like it!" Ronan closes his eyes for a moment and takes a deep breath. "But apparently, she believes she should be dating... and you're better than most options. At least I know you and where you live. You hurt my baby girl... they will never find your body. Got it?"

I just nod my head, unable to find a better response. *Ronan has just told me I should go out with Kinleigh.* I'm half convinced I'm about to wake up and realize my sex-deprived body has fantasized this whole conversation and he has actually called me in here to cut my balls off for staring at his daughter too often.

"You treat her right, Kyle. Don't make me regret this." I just nod again. "Now, get out of my office. I've got work to do and so do you."

Half an hour later, I'm leaning against the bar, still trying to figure out what the hell just happened.

"Kyle?"

Liv's unexpected voice clears some of the fog still swirling around my brain. I twist around until I can see her. She has just entered the bar, pushing one of those foldable strollers with determination in her stride. Ben is strapped down with nylon belts that remind me of the five-point harness you would find in a race car. He's obviously not concerned by his incarceration, judging by his nearly toothless grin and happily kicking feet.

Why in the hell do my friends always bring their kids into the bar? It's a BAR, not the local park! A couple of years ago our friends, Scott and Kelly, had been on a mission to save Logan and Charli's relationship and had shown up at the bar with their twins. Ronan hadn't been happy about it. Some parents have no boundaries.

"Hey, Liv. Why are you here?" I ask, getting right to the point.

"Damn, Kyle... it's nice to see you too! Can't a friend come visit you at your place of employment?" Her eyes narrow speculatively as she cocks her head to one side. "What's going on?"

Charli and Liv are both my friends... and they are both nosy and think my life is their business and expect me to share the details. The difference is, Charli will at least try to be subtle about it. Liv, not so much.

"Not much," I try, doubtful this will appease her.

"Really? Well, okay if you don't want to talk about your life, I understand."

Shit. Here it comes.

I see Liv's dimple appear before she begins her assault. "Let me tell you all about mine. Do you know how hard it is to have sex when you have a baby in the house? Ben won't sleep in his own bed, we've spoiled him rotten, so when he falls asleep we have to sneak out of our room and find somewhere else. So last night, Zac has me up on the bathroom vanity and I hear Ben waking up. I try to ignore him, thinking he might fall back asleep, but then he makes these explosive noises that have Zac cracking up and all I can smell is baby shit and..."

"Okay! No more," I beg in defeat.

Liv smirks. "You have something you want to share?"

"Ronan said I should date Kinleigh."

Liv's mouth falls open as her eyes go wide. "Wait! Hold up... our Ronan? The big guy that owns this bar and scares the shit out of everyone he meets... gave you permission to go out with Kinleigh? Kinleigh Walters? His only child? The daughter that looks for all the world like a Barbie doll come to life?"

I slide onto a barstool and grin at her. "Yeah."

"Well, I'll be damned. Apparently, hell has frozen over and pigs are flying and no one bothered to tell me." She jumps up onto the stool next to mine. "Double damn."

"Da Da Da Da..." We both turn to look at Ben as he tries to squirm out of his stroller. He has a bottle in one hand and something tan and squishy in the other. I think it used to be a cookie.

"Is he trying to say damn?" I ask with some guilt. His mother is the one introducing the word into our conversation, but I can't blame her with the bombshell I dropped.

She smiles affectionately. "No. At least I don't think so. He's asking for his Daddy. Again." Liv crawls down from the stool and squats to get face to face with her son. "Mama. Say Ma-Ma. Please?"

"Dada!" Ben squeals and then stuffs the cookie goo into his chubby little face. That kid is always eating something.

Liv groans. "Ugh! Zac is at his restaurant almost all day while

I'm at home raising our little spawn but all our kid wants to say is 'dada' all the damn time!" She glares at the baby and he grins back her with gloppy brown goo drooling out of the corner of his mouth.

I'm so unprepared for topics like this. I'm also sure she didn't come all the way down here to complain about her 'Mom Problems.' "Why are you here, Liv? Do you need something from me?"

She rolls her eyes. "As a matter of fact..."

I knew it. She wants something.

"I think I have something to give you," she says with a wink.

I make a non-committal noise, wondering what she could be offering.

"I think I have the perfect idea for you and Kinleigh to spend some time together away from the bar and, more importantly, away from Ronan."

"What did you have in mind?" She has my attention.

"I'll get Zac to make you a gourmet meal. You could watch a movie together or have a nice evening to talk and really get to know one another."

I narrow my eyes. "I'm waiting for the catch," I tell her.

"I already checked the schedule and know you don't have to work tomorrow night... you should ask Kinleigh to come over to my house and you guys can babysit Ben for me."

I look at her closely to see if she's lost her mind. "Babysit Ben? You really think that babysitting your kid is the best way for Kinleigh and I to spend some time together?"

"Yes!" Liv lays a hand on my shoulder. "He's so cute and girls get all mushy and shit around babies. She'll think you are responsible and mature. When he falls asleep, I even give you permission to jump her."

I start to laugh. *She's joking, right?*

"But..." Liv puts up a finger, going into lecture mode. "No sex in my bed. That's non-negotiable. Be hygienic about it and remember my kid crawls around on my floors and loves the couch. And for the love of all that is holy... DO NOT have sex in my kitchen. That's so gross! We eat in there! And be sure you..."

"Shut up!" I cover my ears to block her list of "off limit locations for sex," praying she's done. "I'm not having sex with Kinleigh at your house!" I yell.

"You aren't having sex with Kinleigh ANYWHERE!" Ronan yells back as he walks out of his office.

Shit.

Chapter Eight: Kinleigh
Hold Tight & Don't Let Go

"I'm so glad you called," I tell him.

"I'm so glad you gave me your number," he responds.

"Me too, Jeremy." I smile against the phone.

"I'd love to take you out to dinner and maybe catch a movie tonight? Are you available?" I love the slight nervousness in his voice. The last thing I need is another over-confident, cocky jerk acting like he's the answer to every woman's prayer.

"Oh..." I hesitate, hoping he doesn't take my answer as a brush off. "That sounds great but I can't tonight."

"I understand..."

"I really wish I could," I cut in quickly, "but I'm helping a friend out. I'm sorry."

Jeremy clears his throat. "A friend?"

I flop down onto my couch and take a breath. "Yes. I'm baby-sitting her son this evening."

"Babysitting *her* son?" Jeremy sounds much happier. "That's nice of you. I could come over and help if you want. I love kids."

"That's so sweet of you to offer," I assure him, "but this is actually my first time to watch him and since she hasn't met you yet, I'm not sure how she'd feel about it."

"I completely understand. She's a good parent to be vigilant about who is around her child."

It says a lot about his character that he recognizes my concern and doesn't seem at all upset. I really think he is one of the good ones. "Thanks for understanding, Jeremy."

"I do." There's a slight pause. "And... I'm actually a little flattered..."

I frown, trying to figure out what he means. "Flattered?"

He laughs. "Sure. You said your friend hasn't met me *yet*. *Yet* implies she will in the future. It's encouraging, Kinleigh."

I smile at his logic. "I don't play games. I say what I mean," I promise. "I expect the same from the other people in my life."

"I feel the same," he tells me. "So...what about tomorrow? Any more babysitting plans, or charity work, or pressing need to solve the world's hunger problem? Because those are about the only reasons I'm going to allow you to stall our first date."

"Tomorrow would be great," I laugh.

"Good! I can pick you up at seven. Where do you live?"

"You can just get me at the bar." Silence fills his end. "Jeremy? Are you still there?"

"You can trust me, Kinleigh." His tone is measured and calm. "Are you scared to tell me where you live?"

I cringe, realizing I had unintentionally offended him. "No! You don't scare me. I should have explained better. I'm not avoiding giving you my address. I live above the bar."

"Oh! Okay... sorry. I shouldn't have jumped to conclusions..."

His voice is apologetic and I relax.

"No problem. Really."

But is it a problem? He'd understood immediately about my caution in bringing a stranger around Ben. Why would he be surprised about a woman's hesitancy in sharing where she lives? We live in a scary world.

"I really am sorry, Kinleigh. I'm glad you are careful and I shouldn't have reacted like I did. I like you. I like you a lot and I guess I'm still in shock that you seem to like me back. Give me a chance to show you that I'm not a serial killer?"

I laugh. I love how easy he is to talk to. He isn't trying to hide his motives or appear as anything but himself. It's refreshing. "I can do that," I tell him.

"Good."

"I hate to cut our conversation short, but I really need to let you go now. I have to get ready for this evening. But I'll see you tomorrow. Okay?"

"Perfect. Can't wait. Bye, Kinleigh."

"Bye, Jeremy." I push "end" on my phone, thinking about our conversation. He's obviously very sensitive and I feel bad for the momentary confusion but... again, I think how he should understand why I might be reluctant. I just met him and know nothing about him. I feel safe because I know my dad is downstairs most of the time, but if my apartment were somewhere else, I probably wouldn't give him my address this soon.

Looking at the time, I realize I'm going to be late getting to Liv's house if I don't get up and get going. She had called yesterday and asked if I would watch Ben tonight. I'm flattered she trusts me enough to leave her son with me. Ben is also a little cutie and I'm happy to take care of him.

Even though I cut my normal routine down to only an hour,

I soon feel presentable enough to head downstairs. Wearing my favorite pink sweatpants and a V-neck, white T-shirt with the word "Sweet" across the front in pink sequins, I might even look cute. I refuse to think I'm still concerned about how I'll appear if I run into Kyle. I love my outfit, I'm making friends in my new town, and I have a date tomorrow night with a really cute guy that likes me. Life is good.

"Hey, Kinleigh." Leaning against the office door, Kyle is wearing jeans that have seen better days, a black leather jacket, and a sinful smirk that makes my breath catch painfully.

"Hi," I breathe out, trying... and failing miserably... to act like he doesn't affect me. I checked the schedule and know he is supposed to be off. I didn't expect to run into him.

But then why had I come down through the bar? Why hadn't I just used the apartment's other staircase that leads directly outside to the parking lot? I can tell myself I wanted to say goodbye to Dad, but I don't think I believe it.

From behind his back, he pulls out a shiny, round helmet and extends it toward me. "Want a lift?"

"A lift?" I'm humiliated that my voice is so unsure.

He stands up straight and walks over to me. "Yeah. I figured since we are both going to Liv and Zac's house, we should ride together."

"Liv and Zac's house?" I repeat, sounding idiotic.

Wait! What?

My voice regains its normal strength. "YOU are going to Liv and Zac's house too? Why?"

Kyle hands the helmet to me and I grab it out of reflex. "Liv asked if I minded helping you out with Ben." He leans closer and his voice drops to barely over a whisper. "You don't mind, do you?"

"Mind?" Is he asking me if I mind spending the evening with the man that makes my heart melt, my body quiver, and my brain shut down? I need to remember he is also the man that pisses me off and makes me want to borrow from Liv's colorful vocabulary. This is a recipe for disaster, but I refuse to let him know how flustered I am. "I don't mind. It doesn't matter to me at all." I try to think of a way to escape. "But, you really don't have to help me out. I can handle it."

"Oh, I'm sure you can," he answers slyly. "But Ben can be quite a handful. Plus, he will fall asleep eventually and I don't want you to get bored."

"Bored?" *Why do I keep repeating everything he says?*

"And besides... I want you to see my new bike."

Kyle drops the cool façade and now reminds me of a little boy with a brand new toy. I can't help but grin back at him. "You got a new bike? I didn't know you liked bike riding."

"A motorcycle, Kinleigh." He shakes his head at me.

"Oh, yeah... I figured that's what you meant." If he hadn't scrambled my brains with his presence and soft words, I'd have understood immediately what he meant. "So you bought a new motorcycle?"

"New to me. I actually bought it several months ago but it didn't run and it's taken me this long to fix it. She's beautiful. Come see her?" He puts his hand out and I take it. The warmth of his fingers as they slide against mine sends an electric tingle up my arm.

"Okay," I agree. "Let's see her."

His mood is contagious and I catch myself almost skipping as we head out the back door to the parking lot. Parked beside my car is a shiny, orange and black motorcycle. I know absolutely nothing about bikes, but it looks impressive to me.

"It's a 1971 Honda 350 Scrambler," he says reverently.

I run a finger along the side of the leather seat and smile at him. "Okay, if you say so."

"Isn't she beautiful?" he asks quietly.

"She is," I assure him. Turning, I expect him to be staring with adoration at his motorcycle, but instead he is staring at me.

"Want a ride?" he asks.

I swallow hard before answering. "Yes."

His response is a confident smile and wink. *I should change my mind. I should tell him I don't need his help and just get into my own car and go.*

But I can't move. I just watch as he grabs a second helmet from the back of the bike and slips it onto his head before helping me with mine. I watch as he throws his leg over and kicks the shiny beast to life.

"Hop on," he yells above the engine's roar.

Doing as I'm told, I slide my body tight against his back. Unsure where to hold on, I'm glad when he grabs my hands to slide them around his waist far enough for me to braid my fingers together and secure my position. My fingertips twitch with the need to explore the tight ridges of muscles under them, so thinly guarded by his T-shirt where the jacket has fallen open.

"Hold tight and don't let go," he tells me.

"I won't," I promise and lean my head against his back. He pulls out of the parking lot and I love the open motion and the gentle lean as we take curves. It's exciting and freeing.

Liv and Zac live in a nice neighborhood on the outskirts of town and it takes a little while to get there... but not nearly long enough. The feeling of being wrapped around Kyle is sensual overload and I could ride behind him all night.

Well... maybe under him would be even better? I'm in dangerous territory and I know it. He's made it clear I would be the latest in a line of conquests and nothing more. I know that letting my guard down, especially when he's in this mood, will end with nothing but hurt. But when he's this close I feel almost powerless to stop myself.

After he pulls into the driveway and kills the engine, we both remove our helmets but continue to stay seated, letting the searing heat of our contact overrule our good sense.

"Thanks, Kyle. I loved it." And I did. I've never been on a motorcycle before but I now understand the appeal.

He twists around to run a finger gently down my cheek. "I'm glad."

I swallow hard, knowing I need to put a stop to this. "We should go in."

He sighs with disappointment but helps me off the bike. I breathe a little easier thinking I'm in the clear, but then he reaches out for my hand and walks close by my side to the house. My resolve is crumbling and my emotions are in chaos.

Liv jerks open the front door before we even knock. "Great timing!" she says as she hustles us inside and guides us to the living room.

"No! Ben, let go of the kitty!" Liv suddenly screeches and I stifle a laugh as she sprints across the room to rescue a little ball of grey and white fur. Normally I'm sure their cat is nice and fluffy but at the moment, it's a drool-saturated lump of fur.

"Kiki Kiki!" Ben wails with his arms outstretched toward his mother and the poor cat she is protecting.

"No kiki for you," Liv tells her son as she drops the cat into the laundry room and closes the door quickly.

She turns back to face us, where we still stand in shock at the room's entrance. "Ugh! I didn't even want the damn thing. Zac found the kitten crying behind the dumpster at his restaurant and brought her home, insisting Ben needed a pet."

"She's really cute," I offer up as consolation.

"I suppose," she concedes as she walks into the adjoining kitchen and starts to furiously scrub her hands in the sink. "Zac!" she yells in the direction of the hallway. "You were supposed to be watching Ben!"

Zac enters the room, carrying his shoes. "I was! I just had to go grab my wallet and shoes."

Liv shakes her head in frustration before returning to the baby and scooping him up. "Give Mama kisses, Benny-Boo."

"Kiki!" he yells back.

"No kiki, Ben. Please, give Mama kisses bye-bye."

"Num-num?" He asks mischievously.

Liv looks at him with complete adoration. Her son has her number. "You just ate, Chunky Butt! You don't need more num-nums."

Ben looks to his dad. "Num Nums, DaDa?"

"Well..." Zac looks to Liv, pleadingly.

"Ugh! You two are impossible!" She complains but she gives in and gives Ben a handful of snacks that look like little puffed cereal in x shapes. He starts to clap excitedly.

"Num-num!" he says and then stuffs them all into his mouth, making quick work of it even though he only has four teeth.

Liv looks over at me, smiling with pride. I smile back, but I notice Kyle is looking at Ben nervously. Maybe he's having second thoughts about this babysitting thing.

"Ben seems so young to be talking," I comment and Liv beams again.

"Zac gives me credit for that one. He says I always have something to say and it shouldn't surprise anyone my kid does too." She runs her fingers through Ben's dark hair and sighs. "But the little monster still won't say, Mama. His vocabulary is only the three words you've already heard. Dada, kiki, and of course... num-nums. These translate to his father, the cat, and food." She sighs again.

Zac takes Ben from Liv and squeezes in a quick snuggle before depositing him back onto the toy-littered floor. "I'm just thankful some of his mother's more *colorful* word choices haven't popped out of his little mouth," he says with a wink. "But I'm sure it's just a matter of time."

Liv shoots Zac a look that would leave most men afraid to close their eyes at night. "I have a few *colorful* words for you right now," she informs him. Zac's grin just widens. Turning back to me, she starts ticking off instructions. "You have our cell numbers, we should be home by midnight, he's had dinner and his bath and will probably fall asleep soon, I left the numbers for his doctor and poison control on the counter..."

"Poison control!" Kyle interrupts with panic.

"Yeah... just in case. That kid will put anything in his mouth," Liv explains without missing a beat. "Make yourselves at home but..." Liv looks to Kyle. "Remember my rules about where you decide to..."

Kyle interrupts again. "I've got it, Liv!" he practically yells. "Get out of here before you're late!"

"Okay. Okay!" Liv bends down and kisses the top of Ben's head. "Love you, Piglet. We'll be home soon. Be good for Uncle Kylie-Wylie and Auntie Kinleigh."

"Num-num," Ben answers.

When Liv and Zac are finally gone, Kyle sits on the couch and watches as I lower myself to join Ben on the floor. He really is a precious baby and playing with him is soothing. It also takes my mind off that I'm essentially alone with Kyle.

After stacking little wooden blocks, thirty rounds of "peek-a-boo" and lot of sloppy, slobbery kisses, Ben yawns and crawls into my lap to fall asleep. His gentle, snuffling snores are sweet and I love the way he snuggles and roots against me as I run my fingers through his soft, dark ringlets, separating each one and watching them bounce back into place.

"Here, let me get him," Kyle whispers as he bends down and slowly lifts the little boy into his arms. Ben yawns again and then farts loudly...right into Kyle's hand. I start to giggle. "Thanks a lot, kid," Kyle mutters quietly, but I notice how softly he is cradling the baby against his shoulder and how his fingers gently stroke Ben's back.

Watching Kyle tenderly carry the baby away does funny things to my heart. He is a good man with an obvious capacity for love and kindness. Why does he keep pushing me away and acting like an ass?

I finally leave the floor and slide up to the couch. When Kyle returns, he joins me and sits close enough that our legs are touching.

"No problems?" I ask, needing to fill the silence. The baby had been a perfect buffer, but now it's just us.

"He's fast asleep. What should we do now?" Kyle leans in my direction so his shoulder is pressed against mine.

"Kyle...I don't know if we should..."

"Shhh," Kyle whispers and presses his finger against my lips. "We don't want to wake Ben up."

I raise one eyebrow and Kyle grins. Then he turns toward me and brings his head down to feather the softest kiss across my lips. Against my better judgment, I succumb to him, as I always do. I know what will happen. He will make my body come alive and crave his touch, then with a few words, rip my heart into shreds and make me feel stupid for believing we have a chance. I know I need to move away. I need to get up off this couch and tell him I can't do this again. Instead, I kiss him more deeply and take satisfaction in his deep, masculine groan.

In utter defeat, I push him back onto the cushions and slide on top of him. He groans again and I smile. His hands run down my spine and finally come to rest firmly against my backside, pressing and pulling me close against him.

"Kinleigh," he whispers huskily into my ear. "I'm sorry. I need to explain."

I stiffen. Here it comes, his reasons this won't work and an apology for not being what I want him to be. He'll tell me once again that this is a mistake. He's sorry that it can't be more than physical. I pull away, telling myself it's for self-preservation but knowing I'm too far gone for that anyway, but he tightens his arms and pulls me back.

"Don't go," he pleads. "I need to tell you..." The loud wail of "Carry on my Wayward Son," is accompanied by a vibration emanating from Kyle's pocket strong enough for me to feel against my thigh. "Shit! That's Liv's ringtone. She loves that song because of some TV show," he explains. "I have to answer it."

I sit up and move away from him. "Of course. It's fine," I tell him. I hug my arms around myself, rubbing briskly on my own arms to dispel the chill from losing the warmth of his body.

"Hello?" Kyle says into the phone with more exasperation than Liv deserves. I can't tell what she's saying, but her voice is loud and excited and carries through the phone into the quiet room. "Calm down! Say that again," Kyle tells her. "Slowly."

"What's wrong?" I mouth in his direction, but he just holds up a finger, asking me to give him another second.

"Okay, Liv. No problem. I would meet you there, but I can't put a car seat on my motorcycle." There's another pause as he listens. "Okay. Sounds good. I'll be ready."

"What is going on?" I ask as he ends the call.

He smiles. "Charli is at the hospital having her baby. Zac is dropping Liv off at the hospital first then coming home to get Ben. As soon as he gets here, I will take you home.

"Okay, sure," I tell him. "Are you going to the hospital?"

He frowns. "Should I? I love Charli and I'll go see her baby but... I'd feel weird being there for the whole thing." He shudders slightly and I laugh.

"I didn't mean to be in the room with her! I just meant stay in the waiting room to visit with your friends and any family that is there."

"Oh." He looks relieved. "Yeah, I guess I could. I wasn't there when Liv had Ben, but that's because they had me running all over the place to find Zac."

"Zac was missing when Ben was born?" I ask with surprise.

"It's a long story, but he managed to show up in time. It's a good thing too. You know Liv. If he hadn't been there, he'd never hear the end of it!"

I laugh. "True!"

"You want to go too?" he asks.

I look up at him with surprise. "Where? The hospital?"

"Sure."

"Oh...no. Thanks but I haven't known Charli and Logan that long. I'll come after the baby is born."

Kyle scoots closer to me. "They love you. *Everyone* loves you. Come with me."

"Kyle..."

He reaches up and plays with a strand of my hair. "Even if

you don't want to come to the hospital tonight… It will take Zac a little while to get back here… We could just…"

"Kyle, I can't… I…" My phone is the one that interrupts us this time. I pull it out and look at the screen. It's a text from Jeremy, asking me how the babysitting is going.

Jeremy. I have a date with him tomorrow. He wants to go out with me and spend time with me. He isn't just interested in a hook-up. He is the better choice.

"Who is that?" Kyle asks suspiciously.

I smile. "A new friend," I tell him, pulling away.

He scowls. "What friend?"

I stand up. "I'm going to go check on Ben. I'm sure it won't take Zac long to get here."

"Kinleigh…" The pleading in his voice is heartbreaking, but I refuse to turn around. "I need to explain some things to you."

"There's nothing to explain," I assure him.

Chapter Nine: Kyle
You Need A Spanking

"Why is your hair so long?"

I look over and gently tug the end of her long braid. "Why is yours?"

With little arms crossed over her chest defiantly, she cocks an eyebrow at me as if I must be the dumbest guy in the history of time. "Because! I'm a GIRL!" She explains this slowly...and loudly.

"Sophia!" Kelly comes to my rescue and steers her daughter back to the table in the corner of the waiting room where the other kids are playing. "Help Isabella with the puzzle and leave Uncle Kyle alone!"

Sophia isn't diverted that easily. "But Mommy... Ava and Ben keep trying to eat the pieces and now they are wet and slobbery! It's so gross. I want to stay here. I need to ask Uncle Kyle why he keeps drawing on his arms with markers. Dad said he would spank me if I colored on myself again." The precocious child slips out of her mom's grasp and grabs hold of my right arm. "Did you get a spanking?" Her eyes are round and sympathetic and I pinch my lips tightly to avoid laughing.

"Well..." *How do I answer this?*

"That's enough, Sophia." Kelly refuses to let her child get the better of her. She throws me a quick wink and manages finally to pull the child away. I look over and watch all the kids playing together.

Scott and Kelly are longtime friends of Logan and Charli and it's no surprise they want to be here at the hospital for the birth, but I'll admit to being surprised they drug all three of their kids along.

Maybe I shouldn't be, though. They bring them everywhere. The five-year-old twin girls, Isabella and Sophia, are cute, smart, and relentless... like their mom. The youngest, Ava, is close to the same age as Ben and obviously is his partner in crime. As soon as he'd managed to covertly slide a couple of puzzle pieces into his mouth, she had to give them a taste too.

"Times they are a changin'..." I hear when Zac falls into the chair next to mine. I look around and nod my head in agreement. Marriage and babies...it is an epidemic.

"You do realize that at this rate, the munchkins will soon out-number us and the threat of overthrow is real?" I tell him.

"It's almost a certainty," he agrees. "But..." He smiles fondly as his son uses a chair to pull his chunky little body up to stand-ing and then blindly sweeps his hands across the tall table near him, in hopes of finding something he shouldn't have. "It's worth it."

I can't share his sentiment, so I just grunt.

"You don't want kids?" he asks, with no judgment, but a little

69

surprise hides in his question.

"I..." I really think about what he's asking. "I don't know..." I've always thought kids were cute as long as they belonged to someone else. I didn't grow up with any siblings or even cousins. The thought of being responsible for raising a little person and making sure they don't end up some kind of delinquent seems impossibly hard and impossibly scary.

"I've always wanted a family," Zac confesses, "but I think, even if I hadn't been sure at first, I would have been after meeting Liv. With the right woman... well..." We both look up as the woman in question enters the waiting room with a big smile on her face.

"She's here!" Liv beams as Charli and Logan's family and closest friends cheer. "Mom and baby are doing fine. After they get the baby cleaned up and Charli taken care of, we can take turns visiting.

Wow. Charli has a baby. Charli is a mom.

All around the room, people are smiling and crying, peppering Liv with questions. Zac has left my side to scoop up his son into a tight hug and explain that he now has a new baby cousin. Ben couldn't care less and squirms to get back to Ava and the puzzle pieces.

I think of what Zac had been telling me. Does the right woman make the difference? Would I join my friends in settling down and raising a family when she comes along?

Has she already come along?

Last summer had changed something in me. I've enjoyed more than my share of fun with women. I've even had a few real relationships where I was committed to a single person, but life had progressed and I moved on when things didn't work out. Then Kinleigh showed up.

70

I'd been at the bar with Charli and Liv, prepping for opening, when Kinleigh had breezed through the front doors, looking for all the world like some kind of teenage boy's fantasy brought to life. Blonde, blue-eyed, tanned and toned... all wrapped up in tiny white shorts and a pink, cropped sweater... I thought I was dreaming. When she spoke and I got my head out of my ass, I'd been hell bent on pulling out every trick I had to make her mine.

And then Ronan had joined us and her squeal of "Daddy" had brought my machinations to a screeching halt. The most beautiful woman I'd ever laid eyes on was my boss's daughter. Life has a funny way of ruining everything I really want.

I'd been determined to keep my distance. I didn't trust myself. I wanted her too much. I might have survived those couple of weeks if she'd kept her distance too.

She didn't. About three days into her stay, she decided to hang out at the bar during my shift.

"Kyle," she had whispered fervently while slamming against my side and ducking under my arm. "Play along!" she begged me.

"What?" I was confused and my body was already responding in embarrassing ways to the feel of her hot body pressed tightly against mine.

She smiled up at me. "See that guy over there?"

I turned to look in the direction she indicated, trying to see someone that stood out differently from the tightly packed herd of men and women clutching various drinks and moving to the rhythm of the music pumping through the room.

Reaching up, she grabbed my jaw and turned my face back towards her. "Don't look!" she demanded through clenched teeth.

"But you said..." My thoughts had been in chaos.

"Just pretend to be my boyfriend...please?""

I swallowed hard, forcing the lump in my throat to subside.

I couldn't pretend anything with her. It was all real. "Why?" I'd managed to choke out, but just barely. She'd been running one hand across my back while the other held onto my forearm as though I was her life raft.

"There's a guy over there..." Again I tried to look and again she pulled me back. "He is insisting I dance with him."

She had then deftly turned me so my back was facing the crowd with her body pressed tightly against my chest. Her fingers found their way onto my shoulders and up my neck, until landing deeply in my hair. She licked her lips. "I told him my boyfriend wouldn't like it. He doesn't want to take no for an answer so..."

My blood boiled. I grabbed her shoulders and moved her aside, determined to find the douchebag.

"No, Kyle wait!"

I launched myself over the bar, scanning for anyone that could mean her harm. Seeing an overweight prick in an expensive suit leaning against the pool table, letting his eyes become too familiar with Kinleigh, convinced me I'd found him.

Two steps before I'd been close enough to teach him some manners, Kinleigh had jumped between us.

"Not him!" She yelled, in time to stop my fist from finding the sickly pale face behind her.

"Then who?" I yelled back.

She looked around nervously. "Uh..."

"Kinleigh?" I was losing patience. Neither Ronan or I tolerate anyone causing trouble at the bar, but the thought of someone hitting too insistently on Kinleigh had made me furious. I told myself it was on Ronan's behalf since he wasn't there and this was his daughter, but I have a nasty habit of lying to myself when I can't face my own truths.

72

"He left. I saw him leave! You scared him away!" she insisted, pulling me back to the bar.

I tried to cool off and let it go but not being able to confront the asshole had me wound too tightly.

"I'm sure he won't be back. You really scared him."

Making my way back behind the bar, I reached for the bottle of tequila and downed two shots before I could speak. I never drink on the job, but this hadn't been normal circumstances.

"What did he look like? Did he pay with a credit card? Did you get his name?" I started thinking of all the ways I could track him down.

Kinleigh looked sick. "Kyle..."

"Was he here with anyone?"

She swallowed hard and tears filled her eyes. "I'm sorry," she whispered.

"What?" *What the hell did she mean?*

"Don't be mad at me!" I saw a tear slide down her flushed cheek and I started to panic. Had more happened than she wanted to admit? Was she hurt?

"Brooke!" I yelled over my shoulder. "Cover the bar!" Leaving my bartending duties, I put an arm around Kinleigh and pulled her into her dad's office, closing the door behind me. I was shaking with my need to remain calm. "Tell me what happened."

"Oh, crap..."

I put my finger under her chin, forcing her to look at me. "I can't take this anymore, Kinleigh. You have to tell me."

She bit her bottom lip and forced a smile. "Well... it's kind of funny actually..."

I let go of her and took a step back, running into Ronan's desk and letting myself sink onto its edge. "What's funny?"

She starts to pace, with a nervous bounce in her step. "Kyle,

I really like you…"

My heart started slamming in my chest, but I tried to ignore it.

She continued. "I've been trying to get your attention for days, but you don't seem to even notice me."

Not notice her? She could bring a blind man to his knees with her beauty.

"I just thought if I found a way to make you really look at me you might… Oh, God, this is embarrassing!" She covered her face with both hands. "I know you could have any woman that comes in here but…" She peeked between her fingers. "I wanted you to want me."

Her words began to register. "There was no guy?"

"No. I mean yes there was a guy, but he let off immediately when I told him I was with you and he…"

I didn't know how to feel. I felt furious she'd tricked me. I felt guilty she thought she needed games to get my attention. I felt flattered that she wanted me. I felt desire tearing through every cell of my body as I realized we were all alone for the first time.

In one swift motion, I was off the desk and pressing her against the back of the office door, letting my body mold against every one of her perfect curves. I thought I might scare her. I didn't.

Her arms pulled me even tighter, determined to remove any space between us. Without another thought, I brought my head down and lived out the fantasy I'd been imagining since the first moment I'd seen her. Her lips were silk and fire. She tasted of everything sweet and forbidden. Of their own accord, my hands found their way under the edge of fitted T-shirt and we groaned in unison as I managed to unhook the back of her bra. Time

74

stopped.

And then time ground back into gear with a vengeance as someone tried to force their way into the office.

"Kyle? You in there?" Madison had been beating on the door and rattling the handle.

"I'll be out in a minute!" I yelled in frustration.

"Okay! Okay! I just wanted to let you know... Ronan just showed up. He's looking for Kinleigh."

Shit. The whole staff had probably seen us come in here together. Madison had probably just saved me my job... and my life. In a moment of passion, I'd forgotten the perfect woman, ripe beneath my hands, was also off limits.

Kinleigh had stayed two more weeks with her dad. She tried hard to convince me we should be together. It had taken everything in me to deny myself what I wanted most and when she'd left I was convinced her hold over me would fade with time.

Obviously, it hadn't. I still want her more than any woman I'd ever met.

I think back to Zac's explanation and how the right woman changes things. Against my better judgment, I picture a little girl with her bright blue eyes and my dark hair. Or a little boy with her dimples and my love of motorcycles.

I'm a lost cause.

Chapter Ten: Kinleigh

Blow Bubbles, Not Boys!

"She is absolutely perfect, Charli."

The new mother yawns and smiles up at me from her hospital bed. "Thank you. We certainly think so." Charli's hand seeks out her husband's. When their fingers connect, Logan bends down to place a soft kiss on her knuckles.

Gently swaying, I cuddle the swaddled newborn against me and hum softly. Her delicate face is a soft pink and her tiny rosebud mouth is making sucking motions in her sleep. The baby has a light fuzz of soft, dark hair and the tiniest little ears I've ever seen. She's so small and perfect that's it's hard to believe she's real.

"What did you name her?" I ask.

Charli smiles. "Jaci Gail. Gail was my mother's name."

My dad told me that Charli lost her parents when she was young and had been raised by Liv's family. My parents are divorced but I'm very close to both of them and I can't imagine not having them with me, especially for something as important as the birth of my child. "It is a beautiful name," I tell them.

"You just missed Kyle," Logan says as I hand the baby over to him.

"I know. My dad told me that he and Kyle were leaving to get some sleep before tonight's shift. I just thought..." I feel my phone vibrate in my purse and then it begins to ring loudly in the quiet room. "Sorry!" I quickly unzip my bag and hit "decline" to silence the offensive noise.

"Kyle?" Charli asks with a knowing smile.

I look down at the screen. "No, actually it's a new friend," I tell her. "We have a date tonight."

She frowns slightly but covers it quickly. "Oh. Well... have fun."

"Thanks. He's really great." I smile broadly to show her how much I'm looking forward to it. *Am I trying to convince her... or myself?*

My phone vibrates again as a text comes through. I apologize as I look at the screen again. Jeremy is just confirming the time so I respond and tuck the phone away.

"Hey, hooker! I'm back!" We all turn toward to door as Liv barges in behind a huge bouquet of lavender balloons attached to a silver gift bag. "How's my little niece?"

"Perfect," Logan tells her as Liv sets down the bag and balloons in exchange for the baby.

"Naturally," Liv coos at Jaci. "She takes after her Auntie Liv. Don't you, little angel." The baby momentarily opens her eyes, smacks her lips a couple of times, and drifts right back into peaceful slumber. Then Liv notices me. "Hey, Kinleigh. How's Kyle?"

I try to keep the frustration out of my voice. I'm tired of being asked about Kyle. "I really don't know, Liv. I'm just here to see the new family."

"What is all of this?" Charli asks her best friend, indicating the gift at the foot of her bed. "You've already bought her so many things." Charli is smart and I'm sure she is trying to help steer the conversation away from Kyle and me.

It works. "Oh, I found something she had to have!" Liv says excitedly. She reaches into the bag and pulls out a huge plastic bottle.

"Bubbles?" Logan asks in confusion. "Isn't she a little young for that?"

Liv just smiles, hands the baby back to Logan and twists off the lid. Next, she removes the wand and starts a shower of iridescent bubbles that float across the room. "The bubbles are just for effect," she explains. "They are the prelude to the real gift."

With a look of confusion, Charli reaches into the bag and pulls out a tiny white T-shirt. Then she starts to laugh.

"See? It's just what she needs!" Liv says with self-satisfaction, right before Charli turns the shirt around so Logan and I can see the front.

Logan turns red and his lips pinch together before snarling, "Liv! That's highly inappropriate for a baby!"

I look at the shirt. In hot pink letters, it reads 'Blow Bubbles, NOT Boys.'

"Hey!" Liv protests while Charli continues to laugh. "I plan on training her right. She has a lot of stuff to do with her life and doesn't need any boy complications. I'd think you, of all people, would like the message I'm promoting!"

I've known Liv long enough that nothing should surprise me. It might be a little tacky for a baby gift, but I'd be lying if I said it wasn't a little funny too. Logan is obviously having a hard time even thinking of his new daughter in any situation with a boy and I decide to escape before this escalates.

"Well...I really need to get going," I tell Liv and the new parents. "Congratulations again!"

They all murmur their goodbyes and get back to the discussion of exactly what Liv *can* and *cannot* buy for Jaci.

Leaving the hospital, I think about how apparent the love is between Charli and Logan. I also think about Zac and Liv and, how even though they are always harassing each other, they are constantly touching and looking at one another with love. I want what they have. I'm tired of my emotions being a wreck. I need a man that loves me and is worthy of being loved back.

Once home, I jump into the shower and start preparing for my date with Jeremy. I won't lie, I'm one of those girls that takes her time getting ready. I'm even more meticulous tonight, wanting everything to be just right for our first date. I want to give this an honest effort and not let my feelings for Kyle ruin something that has real possibility.

Two hours later, my long blonde hair is a silky, straight sheet down my back, my makeup is perfect and my open-back dress in the palest shade of mint green is adorable. I'm strapping on my nude, heeled sandals when I hear a knock.

I open the door with a smile. "Hey. Welcome to my home."

Jeremy stands in the hallway outside my apartment, dressed in dark slacks and a deep blue dress shirt. Well dressed, but not too formal, he looks great.

Running a hand nervously through his golden hair, he smiles back at me. "Hi. You look beautiful, Kinleigh."

"Thanks! That's sweet of you to say." His manners are impeccable and I could get used to this.

He leans forward and hands me a bouquet of white tulips, wrapped in green florist paper. "For you."

"Oh! I love them!" I take the flowers and motion him into the apartment. "Let me get a vase."

"I know roses are a more traditional gift, but when I saw the tulips, they just reminded me of you."

"I like all flowers," I tell him, "but these tulips are beautiful. I love them!" Grabbing a glass pitcher from a shelf near the sink, I fill it with water and carefully arrange the thick green stems to present the blossoms perfectly. "I'm going to put them on my coffee table so everyone can see them the minute they enter."

"Here, let me." Jeremy takes the heavy pitcher and positions in the middle of the square, low table in front of my couch and then reaches over to squeeze my hand. "Ready to go?"

"Absolutely." The last of my doubt slides away when he doesn't press to stay in the apartment any longer and is eager for our date. His polite manners make me feel very comfortable, so I let him continue to hold my hand as we exit, only pausing to lock the door behind me.

I follow him down the metal stairs that lead to the outside entrance. I had explained to Jeremy exactly where the back stairs were since they are hidden behind the building. I hadn't liked the idea of him using the other set that comes up from the bar's interior, knowing that would be like broadcasting our date to everyone down below. The idea of us having to exit in front of Kyle made my stomach flip uncomfortably.

After our babysitting had ended prematurely the night before, Kyle and I had parted ways. I went home and he went to the hospital. I visited the baby this afternoon after I knew Kyle had left and then it was time for my date. I'd noticed a couple of missed calls from him, but I'm just not ready to talk to him yet. Tonight is about Jeremy. No more thinking about Kyle, I promise myself.

Jeremy offers to drive and we take his car to a nearby Mexican restaurant. Again I notice, with pleasure, how attentive he is. He opens doors, insists I walk on the inside of the sidewalk and asks me a million questions in order to get to know me. He's a perfect gentleman.

"I feel like I've been talking all night," I confess, halfway into our meal. "Tell me about you."

He smiles and sets his fork down. "What do you want to know?"

"I told you my mom and dad are divorced and I grew up with my mom in a small town several hours away, but what about your parents? Are they still together? Do they live close?"

"My mom left when I was really young. I barely remember her. It was just my dad and me while I was growing up. He still lives in my hometown, but I moved to the city for work. Not many opportunities for a computer analyst where I'm from." He takes a sip of his margarita and winks at me. "I'm thinking that move was the smartest decision I've ever made."

I blush at his compliment. He's gone out of his way to let me know how much he likes me all night. "I'm close with my dad too," I tell him. "I was raised by Mom but he was always a big part of my life and I love them both."

"They did a great job," he tells me.

Through dinner and over dessert, we continue to talk about everything. He's easy to be with and I'm surprised when I realize almost two hours have slipped by comfortably.

"Wow... where did the time go? Have we missed our movie?" I ask apologetically. He probably thinks I never shut up. *Why had I talked so much?*

Jeremy reaches across the table and laces his fingers into mine. "It doesn't matter. I've had a wonderful time getting to know you. We can see a movie another time."

"That would be nice." Relief fills me as I realize he wants to secure another date and hasn't been deterred by my monopolizing our conversation all night.

Still holding my hand, he stands up and pulls me to stand beside him. "The weather is great. Want to walk for a bit? There's a great park not far from here."

I gently squeeze his hand. "Sure."

He pays the bill, insisting I can't contribute even though I offered. Tentatively he puts his arm around my shoulders as we walk to his car but I can tell he is waiting to see if I'm okay with it. I am, so I snuggle against his side and I feel him relax.

When we pull into the park a few minutes later, I notice all the people and the well-lit path that runs around the perimeter. I exhale a breath I hadn't realized I was holding. Jeremy has done everything to make me feel comfortable this evening, but I was unsure about ending up in a secluded location with a man I just met.

A light breeze had picked up, so when we get out of the car, he reaches into the backseat for his jacket. I shiver at the contact of his warm hands on my bare shoulders as he helps me into it. "Thanks," I tell him as I slip my hand into his and we join the other people milling around the park.

The path is a fine gravel with solar lights marking it out and there are tall, antique lamp posts at frequent intervals. The heavy scent of roses fills the night air and I can see beautiful gardens in the park's center.

"This place is amazing. I had no idea it was even here," I admit. "I need to get out more and explore my new city."

"Well I'm happy to be your guide," Jeremy says. "Anytime you'd like."

"Good!" I bump my shoulder against his. "I kind of like hanging out with you."

He laughs. "Yeah? I'm glad because I really like hanging out with you."

"So…" I look up and him and grin. "You plan on hanging out with me in the future?"

"Nothing could keep me away," he promises.

Afraid of coming off too serious, too fast, I jump to a new topic. "Well, what exactly does a computer analyst do anyway?"

He ducks his head in mock embarrassment but peaks up through his lashes to wink at me. "It is just as boring as it sounds. I analyze data and operating systems for large corporations and use that information to implement new and more efficient systems."

"Well…" I clear my throat. "That isn't nearly as exciting as my chosen field." I feign a haughty attitude and lift my chin with superiority, but I can't maintain the silly act and start to laugh. "I have a business degree. Nothing special."

"You don't like what you do?" he asks with seriousness.

I sigh. "I shouldn't have said that. I'm fine with my job. I like helping my dad at the bar and there's nothing wrong with a business degree… or a being a computer analyst." I smile and he smiles back. "It's just that…"

"What?" He nudges me. "Tell me what you really want to do."

"It is going to sound ridiculous."

"I doubt that," he encourages.

"I want to bake cupcakes," I admit.

Jeremy stops in the middle of the trail and turns to me. "Cupcakes?"

He isn't laughing so I continue. "Yes. I love to bake. I always have. I dream of one day owning a bakery that specializes in cupcakes."

"Then you should."

"Easier said than done. My parents have always encouraged me in everything, but they are very practical. They felt I needed a degree in something like business to make sure I could always support myself. And I know that one day my dad wants me to take over the bar. I'm his only child and he loves that bar." I take a deep breath and laugh. "I sound like a spoiled brat! Please ignore all of that! I have wonderful parents that want the best for me and a successful business that eventually will be handed over to me. I have no room for complaining. You must think I'm awful!"

"No. Definitely not. I think you are wonderful," he assures me.

An hour later we are back at my apartment door, reluctant for our date to end.

"Can I call you tomorrow?" he asks.

"Yes." I lean forward and give him a warm hug. "I had a wonderful evening."

He squeezes me back and I feel his head resting on top of mine. "Me too, Kinleigh. I think it ranks up there as one of the best nights I've ever had."

I feel myself blushing again. "That is so sweet, Jeremy." I back up a little and look up at him. "I'll talk to you tomorrow."

"Okay," he says, still smiling at me.

I slip inside my apartment. Looking out one last time before closing the door and turning the lock, I see Jeremy is still smiling and whistling as he descends the stairs.

Chapter Eleven: Kyle
Just What Are You Wearing?

"I'm fine, Mom. Really," she insists into the phone again, as I try to pretend I'm not eavesdropping on her conversation. "I've just been busy lately. I'm sorry I haven't called."

Wiping down the bar, I steal glances over at Kinleigh as she paces along with her mother. In a pair of cutoff shorts and a bright yellow tank top, she's hard to ignore. Okay... she's impossible to ignore. Her body is off the chart and I'm weighing the consequences of taking that phone away and hauling her fine ass upstairs.

Kinleigh suddenly stops and begins to smile. "I'd love that! When?" Whatever her mom is promising has made her happy. She starts bouncing lightly and that's when I notice she's barefoot. *Where are her shoes?* I lean forward and look down at her hot pink toenails and the deep tan that seems to cover every inch of her flawless skin.

"What the hell are you wearing?" Kinleigh and I both jerk to attention when Ronan enters the bar. He is scowling at his daughter and I fight to keep the grin off my face. That fight becomes easier when he throws a threatening look in my direction. I have no desire to piss him off and risk losing his recent approval.

Kinleigh holds up a finger in his direction and turns back to her phone. "Hold on, Mom. Dad is here now and asking me something..." She covers the phone with her free hand and smiles patiently at Ronan. "Hi, Dad. I'm talking to Mom. Would you like to speak with her?"

For the first time in all the years I've worked at The Crash, Ronan seems truly flustered. He opens his mouth, shuts it, then opens it again.

"No. Uh... No, I'm good." He rubs absently at the back of his thick neck. "Tell Amber hello. No, that's okay. Never mind. No message."

Kinleigh winks at her dad and puts the phone back to her ear. "Dad says hello, Mom." There is a several second pause and then Kinleigh looks to Ronan. "Mom says hello, too."

"Oh, Okay. Well... I need to talk to you Kinleigh. Can you call her back?"

"Hey, Mom. I'm going to have you call back later, okay?" Kinleigh jumps up to sit on the edge of the pool table and swings her feet as she listens intently to whatever her mom is saying. "Yeah, that's great. Okay. Can't wait. Bye!" I watch with fascination as she tucks the phone, with a pink glitter case naturally, into the back pocket of her little shorts and turns to Ronan. "What's up, Dad?"

He just stands there, a silent mountain. It's awkward and I have no idea what to do. Then Kinleigh breaks the spell by giggling. Ronan's mouth tightens.

"Just what are you wearing, Kinleigh?" He barks out finally and I breathe a sigh of relief, thankful the Ronan I know is back.

Kinleigh looks down at herself and frowns in puzzlement. "Clothes?"

"Clothes?" Ronan explodes. "Those little scraps are not clothes! You aren't at the beach. You are at work." He notices her swinging feet. "And why don't you have shoes on?"

She hops down and goes over to slip her arm into her father's. "Dad, I'm not on the clock yet! Mom called and I wasn't getting good reception upstairs so I came down here." She lifts up onto her tiptoes and quickly pecks his cheek. "I'm about to go change."

"Well..." He sputters, trying to come up with another complaint. "You do that. Now. And don't come down here without shoes anymore. What if there was some glass we missed or something? Idiots break shit in here all the time."

"Yes, sir."

"Okay. Good." Ronan clears his throat. "How's Amber?"

Kinleigh smiles. "Mom is fine, Dad. And she'll be coming for a visit soon."

"What?" Ronan's voice is a mere whisper and he looks pale.

"She misses me. She wants to see my new place and spend a little time with me. She has a long weekend off at the end of this month."

"Oh." Ronan pulls away from Kinleigh and turns to go back to his office. "I have things to do."

Once the door has shut behind him, I come around the bar and walk over to Kinleigh. "What was that?" I ask in awe.

She's looking at his closed door with a grin. "That is how my dad acts around my mom."

"I've never seen him like that. Does he hate her or love her? I really don't know."

"To hear them tell it... They are amicably divorced and wish only the best for one another." She smirks. "I'm convinced they still love each other."

I frown. "Then why did they split?"

Kinleigh sighs. "They got married young, right after my dad enlisted. My dad deployed overseas and it was hard on my mom. It was awhile before I came along and I think Dad thought it would help her loneliness. It didn't. She loves me, but it's not the same as needing your husband to be there. When Dad did come home, he was always so secretive about what he was doing with the military and where he would be and for how long. She just couldn't take it. She never stopped loving him, though."

"He's retired now. Why didn't they get back together?"

"I always hoped they would. I think I still secretly hope they find their way back to each other, but they are both so stubborn. Neither remarried and neither will admit they're still in love."

"Have you tried talking to them?"

She shoots me a look. "Really? Do you know my dad at all?"

"Point taken," I concede. "But what about your mom?"

"She's just as bad. I'm hoping maybe when she comes to visit..." She flashes me that beautiful grin again.

"Playing matchmaker with your parents?"

"Maybe." She blows a bubble with gum I hadn't even realized she'd been chewing. I'm struck dumb by the little pink orb that expands between her full, glossy lips and when it finally pops, I have to swallow hard before I can resume breathing.

"Kinleigh... I want to talk to you," I start, knowing it's time for me to explain some of my past actions... okay... a lot of my past actions.

"Kyle... You *are* talking to me."

I close my eyes and take a deep breath. She isn't going to make this easy on me, obviously. "I need to tell you that..."

We both jump when her phone starts to play the tune of a newly released pop song by one of those boy bands. I really need to expose her to some better music.

She bites her bottom lip and a layer of guilt slides over her features. "Excuse me for a minute." She accepts the call and walks toward the door that leads to her apartment stairs. Before the door closes behind her, I catch her first words.

"Hey, Jeremy. I'm so glad you called."

Chapter Twelve: Kinleigh
Tits For Tats

"Have you talked to Kyle yet?"

"What?" I look up from the stacks of papers on the desk and stare at my dad.

"Have you and Kyle talked lately?" He pulls at the neck of his shirt and avoids eye contact.

"Dad, are you feeling okay?" My father has never willingly discussed boys with me. Kyle and I have to work in close proximity, but recently I've been careful to keep my distance and fend off any approaches at conversation he's tried. Does my dad think I'm letting my work suffer because of my need to avoid Kyle?

"I just...I just thought maybe after...maybe you two might..." He closes his eyes and rubs the bridge of his nose.

"After what?" I ask, stumped as to what on earth he could be talking about. Does he know something about Kyle that I don't?

"Never mind!" He makes a precision turn and marches out of

the office, leaving me more confused than ever.

I think back to the last few weeks and how strange everyone has been acting. I haven't seen much of Charli since she has a new baby, and Liv hasn't been around much but every time she is, I feel like she is watching Kyle and me in anticipation of a show. Madison is the only one that asks about Jeremy. Everyone else avoids mentioning him or changes the topic when I bring him up.

Jeremy. He's great. We've seen a movie, visited a local museum, and have had several more dinner dates. I enjoy spending time with him. He's not pushing me but we've kissed a few times and it's very... nice. Jeremy is a nice guy.

Maybe he doesn't set me on fire or make my heart turn into a jackhammer, but that's not a bad thing! Kyle is passionate and overwhelms my senses. He makes me forget where I am or that anything exists outside the two of us. It's intoxicating and addictive... and bad for me. I need stability and loyalty. I need to trust the man I'm with.

I want to forget that Kyle keeps insisting we need to talk. I need to move past him but after my dad's questions, I can't help but wonder if something has changed. My dad would never encourage talking to Kyle if it would cause me pain. I have to know what's going on!

Newly resolved to clear this up, I leave the office in search of Kyle. The first person I run into is Madison as she clocks in for tonight's shift.

"Hey! We should be packed tonight with that new band playing, Kinleigh. You should ask your Dad to cover a few tables. Tips will be good!" She slips her order pad into the pocket of her apron and smiles.

"Oh, yeah... maybe..." I look around the bar, but Kyle isn't here.

"Who are you looking for?" Madison asks, as she too scans the room.

"Kyle. Have you seen him?"

"Kyle?" She looks confused and pulls me over to sit in a nearby booth. "I thought you were actively avoiding Kyle?"

"I am. I mean, I was. I mean..." I cover my face with my hands and sigh. "I don't know what I mean."

"Well," she laughs. "That much is obvious. Tell me what's going on."

"I don't know. I'm happy dating Jeremy!"

"Why does that sound like you are trying to convince yourself more than me?" she asks.

"Jeremy is good for me. Kyle has made it well known that he doesn't want a relationship and I'm not going to be a hook-up, so I need to let him go, once and for all."

"But?"

"But... Well, he's been acting weird lately. He wants to talk. And now my dad is even asking if I've talked with Kyle and..."

Madison cocks an eyebrow. "Ronan wants you to talk with Kyle?"

"I know! Weird, right?"

"Extremely. Maybe you should. Maybe it will be just what you need to let him go."

I smile sadly. "Maybe so."

"You know..." She lowers her tone, conspiratorially. "Mike and I had issues in the beginning too."

"Really?" I settle in for a story. "You guys are perfect together! I can't imagine problems between you two!"

"I was dating his best friend and then..."

"Excuse me!"

Madison and I both jump as we realize someone had walked

all the way over to our booth without us noticing.

"We aren't open yet," Madison tells the woman.

"I know that," she says as she hitches her purse strap higher on her shoulder. "I'm looking for Kyle."

His name makes my head jerk around to face the stranger. She's attractive with copper-streaked chestnut hair and pretty features, but there is hardness to her face that prevents her from being beautiful. Her skirt is barely long enough to cover the essentials and her white, fitted blouse has only one brave button straining to prevent her abundant chest from escaping.

"Why do you need Kyle?" I ask, too hurriedly, and I see her gaze narrow as she takes in my ponytail and pink sundress before dismissing me with a sneer.

"Who doesn't need Kyle?" she asks with a laugh that makes acid churn in my stomach.

Madison comes to my rescue. "Well, he isn't here yet. Care to leave a message?"

The woman drags her gaze away from me. "Sure. Tell him Tats stopped by to see him."

"Tits? Your name is Tits?" Madison asks with a grin as she stares at the women's chest with amusement.

"Tats! It's short for Tatiana." Her fury is evident, but she's working to control it. "But tell him there's no need to call. I'll see him tomorrow anyway." With that, she pivots on her dangerously high heels and leaves, not waiting for a reply.

Nausea hits me full force. I'd almost talked myself into believing that Kyle had changed and wanted to talk to me about a real future. I'm a fool.

Madison reaches across the table to squeeze my arm. "Don't listen to her. You should still talk to Kyle."

I laugh bitterly. "What's the point?"

Chapter Thirteen: Kinleigh

The Short Answer... I'm An Idiot

"Twenty-two, twenty-three... and twenty-four." I put the last cupcake into the carrier and snap the lid into place. Liv asked me to make two dozen, circus-themed cupcakes for Ben's first birthday. Excited to find red and white striped wrappers, reminding me of a circus tent, I'd made half of the cupcakes s'mores-flavored with mini marshmallows on top, snipped to look like popcorn, and the other half were red velvet with fondant elephants and lions. *I can't wait for Ben to see them.*

Washing my hands and slipping into my shoes, I'm about to grab my purse and Ben's gift when there is knock on my door. Opening it, I see Kyle.

"Hey." His voice is soft, deep and more sensuous than friendly. It makes me shiver lightly. How I wish I could be indifferent to this man. His lazy smile skates the boundary between mischievous boy and predator.

I take a deep breath. "What are you doing here?"

He scuffs the toe of his boot against the door jamb, taking his time before answering. "I thought you might like some help."

I narrow my eyes. "Help?"

"Yeah. Liv called and said you were bringing the cupcakes to the party. I wondered if we could ride together and I could give you a hand."

"How can I bring cupcakes on the back of your bike?" I'm not trying to be ungenerous, but I'm suspicious of his motives and I need to protect myself.

"We could take your car," he suggests.

"Hmmmm..." I look him over. "Are you just trying to get a free ride to the party?" He laughs, and unable to stop myself, I grin back at him. We work together and share several friends. I need to make this work but keep it strictly non-romantic.

"You always assume the worst, Kinleigh."

I decide to let that slide. "If you go with me, you'll get stuck there for the whole thing. No ducking out early. I intend to stay until the bitter end and help with the cleanup," I warn.

Kyle walks past me and into my apartment. Grabbing the cupcake container, he replies, "Sounds more like incentive than punishment."

"Kyle..." My phone chimes and he looks down to where it lies, face up on the coffee table.

"Jeremy is texting you." The flirty smirk is gone and his voice is hard.

Flinching, I immediately feel the urge to apologize but catch myself in time. I have nothing to apologize for. I have every right to talk to Jeremy or anyone else I choose. "Don't look at my phone, Kyle. It's none of your business."

He lips tighten and he doesn't respond.

Swiping my phone from the low table, I hit the home button to bring the text back up. Sure enough, Jeremy is asking if I have any plans today. Typing quickly, I explain about Ben's party. His answering text is so fast the screen doesn't even have time to go dark. Jeremy promises to call me later in the evening. I send a smiley face emoji and then slide the phone to silent mode and slip it into my purse.

"Ready to go?" I ask cheerfully. Kyle just nods and we leave the apartment together.

The ride is quiet, but once we pull up into Liv and Zac's driveway, Kyle turns to me and places his hand on my thigh to prevent me from climbing out of the car. A pleasurable warmth radiates out from his touch and I feel myself almost melting into the seat.

"Kyle?"

"Listen... I need to explain to you... I need to tell you why I..." He removes his hand and runs his long fingers through his dark hair. It's involuntary and undeniably sexy, but I miss the heat of his touch. "Damn," he mutters. "I'm making a mess of this."

He's hurt me enough. I can't sit here and listen again to how he doesn't want the same things I do. Knowing he wants me to warm his bed does funny, fluttery things to my stomach but my heart can't withstand the knowledge that he doesn't want me for more. I have to shut this down... now. "Don't worry about it, Kyle. I get it. Let's just go inside." I unfasten my seatbelt and reach for the door handle.

Grabbing my shoulder, he gently forces me back to face him. "No, Kinleigh. You don't get it at all." I look up into his face, expecting the frown that accompanies his cruel rejections. Instead, I find him smiling. It isn't his sexy, bad boy smirk that makes me want him, even when I know I shouldn't. It's a genuine smile that promises more.

"What is it I don't get, Kyle?" I whisper, confused and scared, knowing how much harder this will hurt if he delivers it with kindness.

"Kinleigh… I'm crazy about you. You're all I think about. You're all I want."

I suck in a deep breath, trying desperately to control my tears. "Wanting me isn't enough. I need more than being wanted. I deserve more than just being wanted."

"I'm so sorry for ever making you think that all I wanted from you was sex. I want so much more. I want to spend all my time with you. I want to laugh with you and hold you when you cry. There is no other woman I want to be with and I sure as hell don't want you to turn to any other man. I want to be your everything."

"I don't believe you," I whisper back.

He winces in pain. "I guess I deserve that. I know I've been awful but give me a chance to show you that's not who I really am."

My responding laugh is bitter and cold. "Not who you really are? Haven't you ever heard that actions speak louder than words, Kyle?"

"Actions?" He actually has the nerve to look surprised. "I've said some things to you that I shouldn't have. I told you we'd never work, even though it killed me to say it. But every time I touched you… it was real. It was me."

My skin tingles as I remember his touch. It's always in the forefront of my mind, ready to torment me. "I didn't mean… I meant… the *others*…"

"Others? What others? There's only you! I haven't been with a woman since I fell for you last summer, dammit!"

Now I'm mad. *Does he think I'm stupid?*

"Really? What about the girls you flirt with at the bar every night?" I yell at him.

"Flirt! All I do is flirt and I don't even want to do that! It's mostly to make you jealous, but you don't seem to even care anymore!" he yells back.

"Just flirting? Really? What about Tits!"

His eyes drop to my chest. "Tits? What about your tits? They're great. I..."

I groan in frustration. "I meant to say Tats! Crap... that skanky woman that came by looking for you. She said she was seeing you the next day and..." Taking in another deep breath, I fight the urge to cry.

"Tatiana?" He leans back in the seat, frowning. "From Zac's restaurant?"

"I know she's your type." I sigh and look over at him, sadness filling every inch of me. "It's okay. Be happy, Kyle." I turn back toward the car door, again intending to get out, but just as before... he stops me.

"She is so far from my type it's laughable," he says. "There is nothing going on between us. Never happened and never will."

"But... she said..."

"The only reason she could have mentioned that she would see me was because I promised to drop a bottle of that new Riesling off at the restaurant for Zac. He said if he wasn't in, I could give it to her because she is the hostess."

"Oh..."

"I told you. There's only you."

My heart beats wildly and I choke back a sob. *How long have I wanted Kyle to say this? Since we first met? But why this turnaround? Why now? And can I trust him?*

"Then why?" I whisper. "Why did you act like that? Why did

you keep pushing me away and treating me like I was nothing to you?"

Kyle unhooks his seatbelt, turns, and leans forward until our foreheads are resting together. "Babe, the short answer... I'm an idiot."

I try to laugh, but it comes out a strangled choke. "Agreed."

He wipes away a tear as it slides a salty path down my cheek. "You are perfect and you deserve more than I can ever give you. The way you make me feel... It scares me. I thought you'd be better off with someone else. I thought denying myself what I really wanted was giving you what you needed." His laugh has an ugly edge. "I also owe your dad a whole hell of a lot and it felt like a huge betrayal of his trust to pursue you. I didn't have a dad growing up and Ronan is the closest thing to one I've ever had. I thought he'd hate me. I thought he believed I wasn't good enough for his only daughter."

"And now?" I ask.

"I'm one lucky son of a bitch. Your dad doesn't want you with anyone... and I can't blame him for it... but he told me that since you seem to have different ideas about this, I'm not too terrible a choice."

I laugh in earnest. "My dad said that?"

"Well... something along those lines."

Thinking about all he's finally admitted, I'm not sure I'm entirely happy with all of his reasons. "So, because of loyalty to my dad, you were willing to sacrifice our happiness?"

Kyle takes a deep breath, places a finger under my chin to raise my face, and looks me square in the eyes. "At first, I was. I just couldn't stand the thought of disappointing him. But the more time we spent together... I was already getting to the point where I knew I couldn't hold out much longer. Even if he'd threatened extreme bodily harm, I would have caved soon and admitted how I felt. It's pretty damn selfish, but I don't think I can live without you, Kinleigh."

I throw my arms around his neck and pull him in for a kiss. A real kiss. A kiss that rids me of all the pain of disappointment and brings on the familiar frustration born of need that can't be immediately satisfied. He returns it and I know real hope for our future together.

We might have continued to make out in the car like a couple of teenagers for the rest of the afternoon if Liv hadn't decided to interrupt up by knocking on the driver side window.

"Hey! You two get out of the damn car," she yells.

Kyle rolls down the window and scowls at her. "What's your problem, Liv?"

Undeterred by his anger, she plants her hands on her hips and begins to lecture. "Well, let's see... We have families arriving soon that may not want to explain a rocking car with fogged up windows for starters. And...all that face-sucking shit is going to heat up the interior of the car and melt my kid's cupcakes!"

"Sorry," I mutter in embarrassment as I open my door and slide out.

"I'm not," Kyle adds after getting out of the car, handing over the container of cupcakes, and kissing the top of Liv's head.

"That's because you're a man," Liv accuses before stomping off in the direction of her backyard.

"Think she'll forgive us?" I ask once she's gone.

Kyle slides my hand into his and pulls me along to the party. "Of course, she will. That bitch loves me."

I laugh and follow him willingly. I think I would follow Kyle anywhere. I didn't realize there was a heaviness in my heart until Kyle admitted his feelings for me and a new lightness takes its place. I feel like one of my angel food cupcakes with whipped frosting and extra sprinkles.

Liv finds multiple opportunities to tease, but it is obvious she's happy about us being together. My dad shows up a little late to the party and just shakes his head in our direction all day. I can tell he is trying to accept the new situation, but it's hard on him and I appreciate the effort. Charli must have hugged us a half dozen times and even started crying when she first found out. Logan blamed it on her "new mom hormones." I think men like to blame everything on our hormones.

Almost four hours later, the cupcakes are gone, most of the guests have left, the kids are passed out all over the living room, and we are finishing the last of the cleanup.

"Thanks again for the cupcakes, Kinleigh. They were delicious," Liv tells me with a contented smile. "Ben couldn't get enough of them."

"I've never seen a kid eat like him," Kyle whispers to me and I laugh. It's true. Ben is a chubby little guy but for as much as he eats you'd expect him to look like a sumo wrestler. It's like his stomach is a bottomless pit. I can't imagine Liv and Zac's grocery bill when he is a teenager.

I pick up my now empty cupcake container and tell everyone goodbye. Kyle throws his arm over my shoulder and pulls me away to leave. This new Kyle is open and affectionate and a constant wonder to me. I can tell his friends are surprised too since they spent most of the party sneaking glances in our direction.

The ride back to my place is nothing like the ride to the party had been. We talk the whole way. We talk about my dreams of a cupcake bakery. We talk about his dream of having a bar of his own. We talk about spending time together and making "us" work.

"Do you want to come up?" I ask as we pull into the parking lot behind the bar.

He smiles at me. "Yes."

Hand in hand, we take the metal stairs that lead to the hallway outside my apartment. At the top, he holds open the heavy metal door and we enter the dim interior. I'm rummaging in my purse for my keys when I hear him curse under his breath.

"What's wrong?" I ask.

Then I see them. A glass vase bursting with dozens of fully bloomed white tulips sits in front of my door. A large heart-shaped card, with my name on it, is stuck onto a long plastic stick, rising several inches above the arrangement.

"Oh," I breathe out as heat creeps up my neck.

"Jeremy?" he asks through clenched teeth.

"Probably," I admit. *I'm a horrible person.* After several dates encouraging his interest, it had only taken Kyle admitting he cared for me to forget about Jeremy completely. I hadn't thought of him once all day.

"You need to let him know that you're with me now."

"I know." I do know, but I'm not looking forward to it. Jeremy is a great guy and we'd had a lot of fun. I don't want to hurt him and I don't want him to think I was leading him on. When I agreed to go out with Jeremy, I had really believed that a relationship with Kyle was an impossibility and I needed to move forward. But, now that I know Kyle feels for me the way I feel for him, there's no contest. Kyle is everything I want.

"Maybe I should go," Kyle tells me and I stiffen.

"Don't do this again!" I grab his arm and squeeze. "Don't run away from me. I choose you, Kyle."

He smiles and bends down to kiss me gently. "I know. I'm not running. I just think you need to call him and tell him it's over...

in your own way. You won't feel comfortable with me sitting next to you."

"Oh." He's right. It would be very wrong to call Jeremy and break things off with Kyle listening to every word. "Okay. Will I see you tomorrow?"

"Absolutely," he promises.

I put my arms around the back of his neck and stretch to put my lips against his. His mouth opens and I disappear into the heat of our kiss. I have no idea how much time has passed when he finally breaks away and smiles down at me.

"I better go. I'll see you tomorrow," he whispers close to my ear.

"Okay. Bye," I whisper back. I stand at my doorway and watch until he's gone. Then I grab the beautiful flowers, go into my apartment, and lock the door behind me.

Once I've set everything down and changed into my favorite pajamas, I grab my phone out of my purse. I'd forgotten to switch my phone back out of silent mode from earlier and I'm shocked to see I've missed twelve phone calls and twenty-four texts from Jeremy. My stomach burns with churning acid as I dial his number.

"Kinleigh?" He sounds happy and a little panicked. "What happened? I was so worried."

"Oh... sorry, Jeremy. I had my phone off. I was at the birthday party and I didn't want to be rude."

I hear him sighing through the line. "You could have put it on vibrate. At least then you'd know I was trying to get hold of you."

A nagging aggravation at his possessiveness starts picking at the back of my mind. "Yes. I guess I could have if I'd wanted to... But I was there to enjoy the party, not talk on my phone."

"Sorry," he says with such sincerity that I immediately feel bad for my harshness. "I was just worried. I wanted to know you were home safe."

"It's okay," I tell him. "I'm home now."

"Good. I'm glad. I was thinking maybe tomorrow we could…"

I cut him off quickly. "Jeremy. I don't think that's a good idea."

"Oh, okay. Maybe the next day we could…"

"No. Hold on a minute. I need to explain something. You are such a great guy…"

"But?" His voice ices over and I take a deep breath, hating that this might hurt him.

"But I can't go out with you again. I'm sorry. It has nothing to do with you. I promise."

"It's that bartender," he says. "You're going out with that low-life bartender, aren't you?"

All pity for him disappears. "You have no right to say that. You know nothing about him!"

"I know more than you think. You can do better, Kinleigh."

"Better? Like you?" I laugh without humor. "I tried to be nice, but I'm done. I'm done with this conversation and I'm done with you. Bye, Jeremy."

I punch the button to hang up When my screen immediately lights up as he attempts to call back, I turn the phone off and throw it into my purse. To hell with Jeremy!

Chapter Fourteen: Kyle

We Have To Eat

What the hell was I thinking? I'm definitely going to fuck this up.

"Kyle... this is perfect," Kinleigh hops off the bike and removes her helmet, releasing a cascade of pale blonde hair, almost white in the brilliance of the summer sun.

Once upon a time I'd been into Charli, had been hurt when she'd chosen Logan over me. Now I'm grateful. I'd cared for her, but it was nothing like this. Knowing Kinleigh has forced me to accept that we don't get to be rationale where our feelings are concerned. Despite knowing that I don't deserve her, I'm not noble enough to give her up. I will selfishly hold on until this crashes and burns... and maybe even longer than that.

Lost too long in thought, I finally snap out of it, when I notice Kinleigh is no longer with me and my bike on the well-worn dirt trail. She's wandered off to the clearing, about thirty yards away. Standing in a shallow beam of sunlight, surrounded by tall, wispy grasses and clusters of pale buttercups, she tips her head back, flings her arms out, and twirls with beautiful abandon. She laughs, loud and unselfconsciously. My heart's response is a deep, almost painful thud of desire.

"You're going to get dizzy and fall," I warn half-heartedly, not really wanting her to stop. I'm enjoying the show, especially the view of her long, tan legs as her skirt flutters higher and higher with each spin.

"How did you find this place?" she asks breathlessly as she wobbles to a stop and sinks to the ground. Sighing in contentment, she lets her upper body fall backward, supporting herself on her elbows, with the rest of her body hidden in the tangled grasses.

I smile. "It's only a couple of miles from where I grew up. My friends and I found the trail here by accident and it was the perfect place to tear up on our dirt bikes. Lots of space, no parents, and no rules."

"Hmmmm..." She opens one eye to stare at me and the corners of her mouth lift slightly. "How many girls did you bring out here?"

I decide to be honest. "None."

Her eyes open wide and she sits up. "Really?"

"Really." Unfastening the buckles on the bike's saddlebags, I pull out the canvas bag I'd packed this morning and a threadbare, plaid blanket that used to be blue but has now faded to a pale grey.

"Why not?" she asks in a teasing tone, refusing to let it drop.

I've never been the type to share my past and it's hard to overcome my natural reluctance, but I've never wanted someone the way I want her. There isn't much I wouldn't be willing to do if she asked.

Spreading the blanket on the ground next to her, I lower my-self onto it and pat the space next to me. She takes the hint and slides closer, sharing the blanket.

"Well?" she prods again.

I sigh. "You're relentless."

"I know."

I try to frown, but my face won't cooperate. I can tell I'm smil-ing. "This place is special to me. I came here to forgot about all the shit I was responsible for at home, all the homework I should be doing, and all the pressure of trying to be an adult while I still wanted to be a kid." I smile over at her. "I liked girls, Kinleigh. I liked them a lot. I dated my fair share of them too... but none of them were important enough to bring here."

I feel her hand on my arm. "Thank you for bringing me."

I answer by slipping my arm around her waist and hauling her even closer. Tipping her head to rest on my shoulder, she kicks her shoes off. We silently enjoy the warmth of the after-noon and the joy of being together.

"What's in the bag?" she finally whispers into the quiet. She reaches across my lap for it, but I gently swat her hand away. She pouts.

"Patience," I whisper back, lifting her hand up to kiss the fin-gers I'd just reprimanded.

Unfastening the knot at the top of the bag, I open it wide and remove three plastic containers with sealed lids, two forks, two plastic cups, and a bottle of wine.

"A picnic!" Kinleigh squeals, flashing me an excited grin.

"Well..." I'm embarrassed. *Shit. I should have done something different. A romantic picnic is predictable. Now it looks like I'm trying too hard.* "We have to eat," I use as explanation.

She doesn't seem too concerned that my plan is so unoriginal. She looks happy.

"So… what are we eating? Did you cook?"

I make a noise somewhere between an incredulous laugh and a grunt of dismissal. "Hell, no! You don't want to eat anything I tried to make. Trust me. Ronan let me grab the wine from the bar and my mom provided the meal. It's her famous manicotti and double fudge brownies."

"Oh my God, that sounds like heaven! Please thank her for me."

I clear my throat as I open the containers. "Would you like to thank her yourself?" I ask softly.

Kinleigh picks up a fork and accepts one of the plastic dishes. "What do you mean?" Her brow furrows as she cuts into the pasta and blows to cool the still hot tomato sauce with ricotta and spinach filling.

"I was thinking maybe later… if you want… we could stop by my mom's house for a quick visit… so you could meet her?" I have never asked a woman to meet my mom.

Her smile is instant and blindingly beautiful. "I would love that, Kyle."

I clear my throat, praying this was the right decision. "Good."

"I know you said your mom raised you…" she says before bringing a sauce covered mouthful to her lips. I watch her close her eyes and enjoy the bite. "Oh my God this is good…" She sighs and I grin.

"Mom loves to cook. She learned from her mother, and my Nonna was half Italian so all forms of pasta were a staple in our house," I explain.

"Lucky you! What about your dad? Was he around?" She scoops up an even bigger bite and pops the whole thing into her mouth.

"My dad left when I was really young. I don't even remember him." I stab my fork into my bowl and slide the tines along the ridges of the pasta.

Kinleigh swallows before speaking. "I'm sorry. That must have been hard."

"You can't miss what you never had," I reply, more harshly than I intended.

"Kyle..."

"It really not a big deal." I smile over at her. "My mom is great and we did fine on our own."

"So she never remarried?"

"She did." It's impossible to hold on to my smile when I think of the asshole that had been my stepdad for a brief... but not brief enough... time when I was in high school. I hate him and the less said about it, the better. "It didn't last."

"Oh," she says, my tone warning her to let the subject drop.

I fish the corkscrew from the side pouch of the bag, hold the wine bottle in my left hand, and expertly open it with a satisfying pop. Without spilling a drop, I fill both of our plastic cups and hand one to Kinleigh.

She takes a sip and smiles. "Good choice."

I grin back. "I'd hope so. Your dad would have run my ass off a long time ago if I couldn't even manage to choose a good wine."

"You are a great bartender, Kyle. He's lucky to have you."

"Yeah..." I look down and fidget with my fork again.

"Did I say something wrong?" Her voice is hesitant.

"No." I look directly into her face and smile. "You didn't say anything wrong. I appreciate it. Really..."

"But..." she drags out, as a question.

"I like being a bartender. It's great and I'm good at it. But, what I really love is helping out with the running of the bar."

"I know my dad really appreciates that too, Kyle. He told me you went back to school a couple years ago to get your business degree and that he made you assistant manager. Does it bother you that I'm helping out now too? I just wanted some experience, but I don't want to..."

I quickly interrupt. "No! I love you working there. I can't do everything and bartend too. We both need the experience. It will help us with our futures. It's great."

"Futures? Do you plan on leaving the bar?" she asks, her voice going up an octave.

"Not anytime soon," I reassure her, seeing the tension fade. "But one day, I'd like to have my own bar. It just makes sense. It's the only thing I know how to do."

"Kyle, don't sell yourself short. You can do anything you want, but if that's really your dream, maybe you should talk to Dad about buying him out. I won't be surprised if he retires in a few years."

I hesitate, scared to admit how much I'd love that. "Maybe... but wouldn't he just leave it to you?"

She wrinkles her nose and I laugh. "I don't want it."

"It's a profitable business, Kinleigh. It has a great location, does steady business with good customers..."

"I know. There's nothing wrong with the bar. It's just not what I want to do. I've told you before."

I shake my head. "Cupcakes? You make the best I've ever eaten, hands down, but there's no way you could pull in the kind of money the bar does."

"It's not about the money."

"That's because you've never done without it," I tell her and her mouth forms a tight line. "I'm not trying to be mean. I just want you to really think about it. My mom worked two jobs and as soon as I was old enough, I worked, just so we could scrape by. Money isn't the most important thing in life, but it sure makes things easier."

She chooses not to respond, instead finishing every bite of the pasta. Then, even though we both admit to being full, we can't resist opening the thick foil packet of brownies. She sighs and I groan as we each bite into the dark chocolately heaven. It's quiet as we eat our dessert but still comfortable and I relax. I'm happy just to be with her.

When we've finished eating, Kinleigh packs the dishes away and I start to stand, thinking she must be ready to go. She stops me by grabbing my shoulder firmly. Without a word, she pushes me until I'm lying on my back with my head almost off the edge of the blanket. I start to ask what she's doing, but she covers my mouth with her hand.

"Sh-h-h-h..." she whispers near my ear and the heat of her breath has me at full attention.

When she climbs on top of me and replaces the hand still on my mouth with her soft lips, I groan and reach to pull her even closer. My hands slide around her back and I carefully roll her so we are now side by side.

Our kiss deepens and her accompanying moans are more erotic than anything I've ever heard. I've always cared about pleasing my partners, as well as myself, but my feelings for Kinleigh add another dimension. I want to do more than satisfy our lust, I want to connect with her on the deepest level. I move my lips along her jawline, down her neck and across her collarbone. She burrows her fingers into my hair and I feel her nails rake over my scalp. Using my free hand, I trace the pattern of her spine, run along the dip at the small of her back, and eventually feel the heaven of her firmly curved backside. She hitches her long leg over my hip and I catch it under her knee, feeling the silky smoothness of her warm skin. I love that she is wearing a skirt and I can slide my hand along her leg without any barrier.

"Every inch of you is perfect," I tell her and I mean it.

She giggles softly. "You haven't seen every inch of me, Kyle."

"I intend to," I promise with a growl.

"Good."

I bring my hands up between us and start releasing the small buttons that close the front of her shirt. Every inch of newly exposed skin gets a line of gentle kisses before I move on to the next one. When the last button is unfastened, I slide my hands under it and around her back. A quick tug in the right direction on her bra strap and I've removed the last impediment. She wiggles out of the newly opened clothing and I jerk my T-shirt over my head in one, lightning-fast motion. Her bared breasts are fire against my chest, I feel singed everywhere our skin makes contact. I kiss her again.

Cupping her soft breast in my hand, gently kneading its fullness, I bring my mouth down to tease the tip. Kinleigh arches fast and hard against me.

"Kyle..." Her breath is coming deep and ragged now, matching my own.

"I know," I tell her. I want this woman more than I've ever wanted anything in my life.

As I continue to worship her perfection, her hands begin roaming more freely over my skin and my muscles tighten with the sheer pleasure of her touch. When she starts to unzip my jeans, I almost lose control.

Sliding my hand under her skirt, I slip a finger under the elastic of her panties, ready to finally make this happen. I expect

112

her to draw closer... instead, she abruptly pulls away and grabs for her discarded shirt.

"What's wrong?" I sit up, trying not to panic. "I thought you wanted..."

"Did you hear that?" She is covering herself and looking around the clearing. I follow her gaze but don't see anything.

"Hear what?" I ask in irritation, reaching to pull her down with me again. "There's no one here but us."

She resists. "No! Listen. I hear an engine."

She's right. If I hold my breath to silence my frustrated gasps for air, I can hear the distant whine of an engine. "Shit."

"I think someone is coming! Get dressed." Throwing my T-shirt at me, she ruins a perfectly good view of flawless skin and high, firm breasts by putting her bra and blouse back on.

Just as she fastens the last button, two dirt bikes break through the trees that border the path opposite the trail we had entered from. Fumbling around for her shoes, she looks like an adorable mess with her wild hair and flushed cheeks. I've managed to zip my pants, even though thanks to her they are much tighter than they had been, but my shirt is still balled up in one hand as I watch the intruders come barreling across the field.

Noticing us, they slow their approach. They are still a good distance away when they stop. A couple of teenage boys with bad skin and identical smirks cast looks between Kinleigh and me and nod to one another in understanding.

"Hey," the taller one yells. "Sorry to interrupt your... fun." They both laugh.

Jumping up, I start for them, but Kinleigh pulls my arm to stop me. "They're just kids, Kyle. Don't worry about it."

"Fine," I mutter, reaching down to grab our blanket and bag. "Let's just go."

Walking away from them, and toward my bike, the boys' next words carry across the distance and I clench my fist, desperate to control my temper.

"He was totally about to get some!" one says with knowing authority.

"Yeah, and did you see how hot she is? We should have hidden and watched. I'd love to see *more* of her," the second responds.

I want to go kill the little shits. I'm worried Kinleigh is embarrassed but obviously she isn't. She's laughing and shaking her head with amusement I don't share.

"Why the fuck are you laughing?" I explode at her. She laughs harder.

"Because they're just little boys acting like little boys. Don't you remember being that age? What would you have done if you'd come across a couple, in the middle of nowhere, about to do some very naughty things?"

She has a point, but I don't want to admit it. We both know I'd have acted the same and probably worse. It all feels very different when the teenage lust is directed at my Kinleigh though.

"It's getting late, anyway. Let's go see my mom," I concede grumpily.

Again she laughs.

Chapter Fifteen: Kinleigh
Such A Good Boy

Pressing my cheek against his back, with arms wrapped tightly around his rock-hard body, I sigh with contentment. I never thought of myself as a "motorcycle girl" but I could get used to the security I feel, so close against Kyle's strong warmth, and the dangerous thrill of high-speed motion in the open air. The sun is bright and unrelenting but riding a projectile causes the day's gentle breeze to become a gale force wind that cools as it whips the portion of my hair that falls below the helmet.

I know his mom still lives in the house he grew up in, only a short distance from where we had our picnic, so our quick arrival isn't a surprise, but I would be content to stay like this forever. With Kyle, I feel dangerously excited and completely safe. I trust him.

"Almost there," he yells back at me before leaning into a sharp right turn. I let my body mimic his movements, enjoying the thrill of the bike tipping closer to the ground. Once we straighten back up, I notice we are in a neighborhood lined with small, older homes. The sun is disappearing into the horizon and the far-spaced streetlights respond, casting long circles of amber light. Reaching the end of the street, he pulls into the gravel driveway of the last house on the left. Like the others around it, the one-story home is a box with lap siding, a square front porch covered with a steep gabled roof, and a postage stamp yard. Unlike most of the other houses, it has a fresh coat of paint, perfectly trimmed hedges, and a riot of orange and pink flowers overflowing from window boxes.

"This is where you grew up?" I ask. "It is adorable."

Kyle flinches but smiles. "Great. I love being associated with adorable." He throws his arm over my shoulder and we walk up to the front door. Before he can knock, the door opens.

"Kyle!" A petite woman barrels out and I step aside as she grabs her son into a warm embrace. She has dark hair, generously sprinkled with silver and neatly pinned at the back of her head. Deep brown eyes that look as though they've seen a lot but refused defeat, crinkle with pleasure. Even though time has left its mark on her, it's obvious where Kyle's good looks came from.

"Hey, Mom." Kyle's voice is soft and respectful, completely devoid of his usual sarcasm. He loves this woman and she obviously adores him.

Finally letting go of her son, she turns to me with a large smile and tears in her eyes. "You have to be Kinleigh." She swats Kyle on the arm, playfully. "You said she was beautiful, but that doesn't do her justice."

Kyle looks at me. "I know."

Putting my hand out, I step toward her. "It is so nice to meet you, ma'am."

"Oh honey, none of that!" She folds me into a hug, refusing the idea of a simple handshake. "Please call me DeAnna. And come on in. Let's all go inside."

Following her into the house, we pass through a spotless living room to enter a bright kitchen with white cabinets, large windows framed by yellow checked curtains, and a round, formica-topped table that reminds me of retro diners.

"Sit down and let me get you something to drink. Are you hungry?" DeAnna bustles around, pulling glasses from a drying rack next to the sink.

"Thanks, Mom... but we just ate, remember? I'll get your bowls back to you before we leave."

"Did I pack enough? You aren't still hungry? I have more brownies..."

Kyle puts his hands on her shoulders and steers her over to sit next to me at the table. "Mom, just sit down. You packed more than enough food and I can make us something to drink."

She lovingly pats his hand, still resting on her shoulder. "Okay. Thank you, Kyle." When he goes to fill the glasses with ice cubes, she turns to face me. "I'm so happy to meet you. You just don't know how happy it makes me."

"I feel the same," I assure her.

"My Kyle is such a good boy. He deserves someone special."

Kyle groans. "Mom..."

"You do! You work so hard and still find time to take care of my house and yard and help me with everything. Don't be embarrassed that I'm proud of you!"

He removes a pitcher of tea from the refrigerator, fills the three glasses, and then joins us. "I'm not embarrassed," he tells her. "I just think you exaggerate."

"Nonsense!"

I laugh at their gentle disagreement and take a sip of the sweet, minty tea. "I want to thank you for the food. Kyle told me you made it and it was delicious."

DeAnna smiles with pride. "Well... it was nothing. Just a simple recipe my mother taught me. I'm glad you liked it."

"I did," I assure her. Kyle smiles at me, silently thanking me for my kindness. I want to tell him that my compliment is truth and I think his mom is wonderful.

"Kyle tells me that you make the best cupcakes he's ever had."

"Oh..." I feel myself blushing.

"She does." Kyle reaches across the table to squeeze my hand.

"I don't know if they are the 'best', but I do love baking and..."

DeAnna interrupts gently, "If Kyle says they are the best, then they are."

I laugh at her complete faith in everything her son says. Here in this house, across from his mother, it's hard to believe Kyle is the hot bartender that loves to flirt with every female that comes through the bar's front door. He pushed me away for so long, convinced he wasn't good enough for me, but all I see is a mature and responsible man that works hard and takes care of his family. I'm lucky to be with him.

After answering all of DeAnna's questions about my life and hearing lots of endearing stories about Kyle growing up, we regretfully explain that it's time for us to go. She's disappointed but understanding as she walks us to the door.

Before we can leave, DeAnna grasps both of my hands in hers and smiles at me. "Thank you so much for coming to meet me today, Kinleigh."

"Thank you for having me."

"You take good care of my Kyle. He hasn't always had it so easy and I want to see him happy. I believe you are just what he needs," she tells me, finally releasing my hands.

"I'll do my best," I promise. I give her a quick hug, feeling a connection with the small woman. We both love her son.

"Well..." Kyle cuts in. "If you two are done talking about me like I'm not even here..." We both laugh. "We really do need to get back before Ronan sends out a search party. Bye, Mom." He hugs her on the front porch and we head for his bike.

As we drive away, I turn and see she is still standing on the porch, leaning on the door frame, watching us go.

Chapter Sixteen: Kinleigh

Kinleigh, Kinleigh Nicole, Kinleigh Nicole Walters

How do I always end up with the shopping cart sporting wonky wheels? It takes all my strength to steer the cart onto the aisle with baking supplies. Turning left is no problem, but every right turn requires me to lift the back end and force it in the correct direction. Luckily, I just need to grab a bag of confectioner's sugar and some vanilla extract for my grocery shopping to be complete. I plan to try out a new recipe tomorrow for Kyle. Making Corona cupcakes with lime frosting might be the final push to convince Dad to let me offer them in the bar.

The sugar doesn't present any problems, but when I try to get the vanilla, I can't find it. After several minutes of slowly looking over the rows of tiny bottles, I realize the pure Madagascar vanilla is on the top shelf, a few inches beyond my reach, even when on tiptoes.

"Crap," I mutter, wondering if I'll be kicked out of the store if

I use the bottom shelf as a step.

"Here. Let me help you," a deep voice says from behind me.

I turn to thank my rescuer but instead of seeing the expected helpful stranger, I'm looking at a cold version of a smile I recognize. *Jeremy.*

"Oh..." I flinch as he brushes against me to retrieve the dark, glass bottle of vanilla. I know he isn't some villain out to get me... but our last conversation hadn't gone well and I've been ignoring his texts and calls since then. "Thank you."

"Of course. Happy to be of assistance." He's still smiling but it doesn't reach his eyes and there's a nervous tightening in my stomach.

"Well... I really need to be going." I start to push my cart around him, determined to escape the grocery store as quickly as possible.

"What's the hurry?" he asks, stepping to block me.

"I have things to do."

"Things to do with the bartender?" His voice is quiet but hard.

"That's none of your business," I fire back.

He smiles. "I've called you and left messages."

"I know... I'm sorry. I just didn't think we really have anything to talk about anymore."

"If you say so." He looks into my cart, picks up a small bag of limes and then sets it back down.

"I have to go, Jeremy," I insist through clenched teeth.

"Of course." He steps to the side and smiles. "It was so nice running into you, Kinleigh. I hope to see you again soon."

Without saying a word, I push the errant cart as fast as I can to the checkout, happy that I find a lane with no wait. Making my way across the parking lot with my bags, I keep checking over my shoulder, eerily convinced Jeremy is lurking somewhere, watching me. I know I'm just being paranoid. I hurt his feelings so he isn't showing the best side of his personality but I don't have any real reason for concern. I need to calm down and let his strange behavior go. It was a total fluke that I ran into him and I'll probably never see him again.

Driving home, I turn the radio up and sing along to an awesome new song that embraces the idea of girl power. By the time I've carted my groceries upstairs and put them away, Jeremy is a distant memory and I feel silly for overreacting in the store. It's time to get to work.

The bar is coming to life as the day slides into evening and most people's work day is at a close. Kyle is pouring drinks and making small talk with everyone along the length of the bar. As usual, I notice a lot of women desperate to get his attention. He is always polite but never encouraging and I warm with pleasure every time he shoots me a special smile or quick wink.

"Well, well, well... looks like someone has tamed the beast," Madison laughs as she passes me with a tray full of drinks. I just grin in acknowledgment.

Once she has delivered the orders, she meets me near the office doorway where I'm looking over the crowd. "You look happy," she tells me.

"I am."

"I'm a big fan of our Kyle... and I think you are great, Kinleigh. I want nothing but happiness for both of you but be careful, okay? I just don't want you to get hurt. It wouldn't be intentional but..."

"I understand," I assure her. "Thanks but we are in a really good place and I believe it will all work out perfectly."

She slides an arm around my shoulder and gives me a quick squeeze. "You might be right." Winking at me, she says, "I almost forgot! Look what I found on one of my empty tables." She reaches into her apron pocket and hands me a cocktail napkin.

I'm confused. "What is this?"

"It was just laid there, under an empty beer bottle. Kyle must have done it, right?" We both look over at Kyle, but he doesn't notice us.

Smoothing the napkin out on my hand, I see it has writing all over it. Almost every inch is covered with my name. There is "Kinleigh", "Kinleigh Nicole" and even "Kinleigh Nicole Walters" in cursive and print, small and large, in every direction.

"Sure. He must have," I tell her, but I'm not convinced.

"Who else would have done it?" she asks, picking up on my unease and sounding concerned.

"I don't know... It's just that..."

"Just what, Kinleigh? You're freaking me out."

"When would he have put it on the table? He's never come from behind the bar," I point out.

"I assumed he asked someone to put it there for you to find."

"On your table?"

"He knows we are friends," she says and I see the truth in her assumption.

"Yeah, but..." I take a deep breath, thinking. "When would he even have time to write all this?"

"Maybe before shift started?" Madison looks around the bar as if answers will present themselves. She is seeing the holes in her theory.

"Maybe. I'm sure you are right," I reassure her. "I know you need to get back to your tables."

"You okay?"

"Absolutely." I smile to add weight to my words.

Madison leaves me to check on her customers and I scan the

bar. It's a dim atmosphere but there is enough light to see everyone clearly and I don't see anything suspicious. What am I really looking for anyway? Jeremy had made me nervous earlier at the store and I'm letting that cloud my judgment. The napkin has to be a sweet gesture from Kyle. I fold it up and slip it into my jean's pocket, determined to ask him about it later.

Chapter Seventeen: Kinleigh
No "Cha Cha Slides"

"You look beautiful," he whispers against my neck and a round of shivers shimmy down my bare spine. My simple black cocktail dress leaves my entire back exposed.

"Thank you," I whisper back as I sit down in the chair he's pulled out for me. "You look beautiful too, Kyle."

He laughs. "Beautiful? Not exactly what I was going for."

"Trust me... It's a good look," I assure him, letting my eyes take in his dark suit, dress shirt without a tie, and the neat way he's pulled back his hair.

"Well, I'll admit I'm enjoying looking at you a little too much. You, Princess, are a distraction. Today is supposed to be about Liv and Zac and I think you stole the show."

He's crazy. Liv and Zac's wedding had been flawless. There hadn't been a dry eye in the church when they'd exchanged the vows that had included a commitment to Ben and any future children they would share. Even though Liv loves to joke about everything, she'd taken her ceremony very seriously. Now that the reception has kicked into full gear, though, the Liv we all know and love is back in full force.

"They look happy." We both look at the newlyweds as they begin their first dance as a married couple.

Our table suddenly shakes, startling us both as my dad leans heavily on the far edge and lowers himself into one of the delicate gold chairs, messing up the ivory satin bow that wraps around it. "How long is this thing supposed to last?" he asks gruffly.

I laugh. "Aren't you having fun, Daddy?"

"Weddings just aren't my thing." He pulls to loosen his tie. "At least we know the food will be good."

Zac is an amazing chef and the reception is at his restaurant, so we are all anticipating the meal.

"Why didn't you and Mom have a big wedding?" I ask, curious to see how he'll answer. Mom always tells me they hadn't thought it was important at the time, but her expression contradicts that explanation.

"What difference does it make now, Kinleigh?" He takes a sip from his wine glass and avoids my gaze.

"I want to know."

He sighs heavily. "We didn't have a lot of time to plan. I was about to be shipped off. Plus, I didn't have much family to invite and Amber's folks..." He takes another drink. "Well, they thought your mom could do better. It just didn't seem like a good idea. I really thought your mom was okay with us just going down to the courthouse too... until we had our first real fight."

I notice Kyle really looking at my dad. Surprise is evident, but he's also paying close attention to what my dad isn't saying. It's obvious the lack of a wedding ceremony had caused some real problems.

"I'm sorry," I whisper. Dad seems to understand that I'm sorry it had been a problem between him and mom, but also for bringing it up today and making him relive it.

"It's fine. That was a long time ago. Amber knows that if I had any idea, she really wanted all this…" He swings his arm wide to indicate the room full of guests, decorations, and celebration. "I'd have made it happen for her."

I come around the table to give my dad a hug. "I'm sure she does."

The DJ announces that the floor is now open to everyone and guests get up to join Liv and Zac in the center of the room.

"Let's dance, Dad." I try pulling on his thick arm, encouraging him to join me.

He won't budge. "No, thanks. This is for you, young people. And besides, you wanted *him* to be your boyfriend so badly," He nods his head in Kyle's direction. "And this is what boyfriends are for. Make him dance with you!"

I laugh. "Okay, fine. But before this is over, you have to dance at least once. If you don't want it to be with me, then you better find someone." I scan the room for potential partners. "I think Zac's aunt is single. Have you met her? Ginger's sister, LeeAnn? She's really pretty and…"

"Enough!" he growls. "I don't need my daughter trying to set me up with anyone."

Throwing my hands up in defeat, I go back to Kyle. "Shall we?"

He stands and slides his arm around my waist. "Definitely."

"I'm watching and I better see some daylight between you too," my dad warns. "None of that 'dirty dancing' crap."

I laugh, but Kyle shakes his head. "He doesn't make this easy."

Sliding my arms up behind his neck, feeling his arms encircling my waist, I lay my head on his shoulder. "I'm worth it," I remind him.

I feel the chuckle that reverberates through his chest. "Yes, I think you are."

Swaying to the music, I close my eyes and let him lead. He's a good dancer and I feel a contentment settle over me. I'm happy. There is nowhere I'd rather be right now and no one I'd rather have holding me.

We dance through several slow songs, but Kyle draws the line at 'the cha cha slide.' It's a staple at most weddings, but he can't be convinced to give it a try, so we join Madison near the bar.

"You guys looked great out there!" She gives me a hug as her boyfriend shakes hands with Kyle. Mike is of average height and build, and has an unremarkable face... until he smiles. Then his face transforms with a mischievous sparkle in his eyes and a contagious joy. And it is obvious he's crazy about Madison, so of course, I like him.

"Thanks! I love to dance," I tell them. "And the DJ is really good."

"Until he decided to play this shit," Kyle mumbles.

Mike laughs. "I agree. Why do women like all these line dances? Too complicated for me."

Madison cocks an eyebrow in his direction. "All dancing is too complicated for you. You just sort of slowly move around when I force you onto the floor."

He hands her a new glass of champagne. "But I have other skills to make up for my lack of dancing ability," he says confidently with a wink and she actually blushes.

"Hmmm... Come to think of it, you are rather good at..."

Kyle starts tugging on my arm and I get the hint. I turn with him to leave when Madison's next words stop me.

"What in the hell is *he* doing here?" She looks with concern toward Kyle and me and then focuses behind us.

I feel Kyle's muscles tense and he squeezes my arm a little too firmly, causing me to wince. Turning together, we see Jeremy standing on the opposite side of the dance floor, smiling in our direction.

"Why is he here?" I ask, shocked at his appearance at my friends' wedding. "He doesn't even know Zac or Liv!"

"I'm about to give him a good reason to leave," Kyle says with dangerous quiet.

"Kyle, there's no need to cause a scene. He hasn't done anything."

"I don't trust him."

I don't want to admit that Jeremy is making me nervous too. It's true that he hadn't taken my breaking things off very well and he'd said some unkind things. He's also been blowing up my phone constantly and I've had to block his number. But I still feel guilty for letting him think we had a chance, so I hadn't shared my concerns with Kyle. Should I tell him about the grocery store run-in? The hatred on his face convinces me to hold my tongue.

"I'll go talk to him," I offer. "Explain that I would prefer he leave."

Kyle looks at me. "No. I want you to stay away from him. Let me handle this."

I love that Kyle feels protective, but I'm a big girl and won't be told what to do. "I'm afraid of how you might decide to handle it!"

Then Jeremy's loud laughter reaches us and my head jerks up to find him. He's helping Brooke up from her chair and leading her onto the dance floor. She's leaving no doubt that she loves his attention and she pulls him in close and grinds against him. What she doesn't realize is he's watching me the whole time.

"He came with Brooke?" Madison asks as she steps closer to my side. "She told me she'd met a new guy during her shift last weekend and she'd ask him to be her date for the wedding, but she never said his name."

"Oh, well... I hope they are happy and..." my voice trails off and it feels like ice water is coursing through my veins. Had he planned this?

"Did she know you were seeing him before?" Madison asks.

Kyle's had enough. He leaves us and goes back to the bar for another drink. I feel so bad. Jeremy is such a sore point between us.

"Sorry..." Madison mutters in apology.

"No, it's fine. Kyle doesn't like it... but it happened. He knows it's over now and he has nothing to be mad about. And it is possible that Brooke never knew I went out with Jeremy. We didn't date long and we never hung out at the bar."

"Okay," she concedes, "but even if she never knew, why would Jeremy come to the bar and pursue her? He knows she works for your dad and you'd know each other."

"It has to be a coincidence," I say unconvincingly. "He isn't banned from the bar just because I don't want to date him. And Brooke is a pretty girl so it's natural he would ask her out."

I feel Madison's hand come down on my shoulder. "There isn't anything natural about this situation, I'm afraid."

She's probably right. Just when I've convinced myself to walk over and confront him, he leads Brooke off the dance floor, whispers something into her ear, and then waits as she retrieves her purse from their table. Sliding his arm over her shoulders, he throws a quick wave in my direction before they leave together and I'm finally able to release the breath I hadn't realized I was holding.

Chapter Eighteen: Kyle
Murder Charge

I will hunt down the sorry son of bitch that did this... and kill him.

"Kyle? What's wrong?" Kinleigh comes out of the office and immediately joins me at the bar as I pour myself a drink and slam it back.

"It took me months of work to make her perfect!" I pour another drink. "And someone dares to fuck with her?" It goes down as quickly as the first shot had and I enjoy the burn of it.

"Kyle." Kinleigh lays a hand on my arm and stops me from pouring a third drink. "Tell me what happened."

"The Scrambler...my bike..." I let my voice trail off and think about the carnage I just discovered.

A few minutes ago, after hours of working on some new advertising promotions for the bar, Kinleigh's stomach had started voicing hunger complaints loud and clear. Being the decent guy that I am… and fucking starving myself…I'd offered to run down the street to the new Thai place for some takeout. Leaving her alone in the office, I'd gone out to the back parking lot to jump on my bike. What I found had made me sick.

"What happened?" she asks again, looking more panicked than the situation probably warrants. My anger is justified, it's my bike after all, but I hadn't meant to upset her.

"Some asshole knocked my bike over, kicked a huge dent in the gas tank, and busted my mirrors." It hurts to even say it.

"Oh…" She responds, nervously playing with my discarded shot glass. "Could it have been an accident? Like, maybe it fell over?" She's acting like she is somehow responsible for the damage. Does she feel guilty that it happened behind her dad's bar? It isn't her fault, but someone is to blame. There are assholes in this world that take pleasure in ruining what they don't have themselves or just to see if they can get away with it.

"No. This damage was deliberate and if I find out who is responsible, they're dead!" My anger is escalating again and right now a murder charge doesn't seem like the worst thing. "We need to install security cameras out back!"

"I'm so sorry!" Kinleigh starts to cry and I feel like shit. The security camera remark had probably added to her guilt. Maybe my anger is scaring her too.

I fold her tightly into my arms and kiss the top of her head. "You don't have anything to feel sorry about. It's not your fault. I'm pissed but I'll get over it."

Now she starts to sob even harder. "Kyle…"

"Sh-h-h. Don't be upset. I'll fix it. It's nothing I can't take care of." I hold her shoulders and push her back far enough to see into her face. "How about tomorrow you come over and hang out while I work on it? We're both off and we'll have the whole day."

Kinleigh wipes at her eyes and sniffs loudly. "Okay. Your apartment?"

"No. My tools are all in my mom's garage. I don't have anywhere to store them at the apartment. I'm going to call Logan and see if I can borrow his truck so I can haul the bike over there," I explain.

She smiles softly. "I'd love to see your mom again."

"Actually..." I smile back at her. It's amazing how this woman makes me forget how pissed I was only seconds ago. "My mom is away all weekend, visiting a friend out of town. We will have the place to ourselves."

"Oh... that sounds promising."

"Yes, yes it does," I agree before dipping down to kiss her. Her enthusiastic response makes me tighten with desire. We've had too many interruptions. We will be alone all day tomorrow and this is going to happen.

Chapter Nineteen: Kinleigh

You're Mine. Only Mine.

"Thanks a lot, Logan. I appreciate the help. You know, in the past I might have told Charli, once or twice, that you were a douchebag lawyer and she could do better... but I take it all back," Kyle says with a grin as he extends a hand in thanks.

"Well, if we are being honest... I might have told her you were a man-whore that didn't deserve her, so..." Logan accepts Kyle's hand with a big smile and pumps it firmly. Then he looks in my direction. "Seems we were both wrong and things ended up as they should for all parties involved."

"Okay, boys...wrap it up!" I cut in. "We've got stuff to do today." Standing around while they apologize for their history of distrust is a torture I can do without. Listening to their self-congratulations on their choices in women is even worse. Let's be honest. It hadn't been their choices. Charli and I are both determined when we want something.

Logan laughs. "Bye, Kinleigh." He gives me a brief, one-armed hug and I squeeze back.

"Bye. Please tell Charli hello for me and give sweet little Jaci a kiss. I can't wait to see her again. She's such an adorable baby."

Logan beams with pride. "She is perfect."

"I'll come see her soon. And thanks again for helping get the bike. Your truck and your muscle are both appreciated."

"I'll happily accept payment in the form of cupcakes," he tells me with a wink.

"Deal!"

Kyle and I stand side by side at the front of his mom's garage as Logan backs out of the driveway. We return his wave when he pulls out into the road and leaves us alone. All alone...for the entire day.

"So, where do we start?" I ask, turning away from the departing truck to face Kyle.

"We?" I watch as his gaze takes in my carefully braided hair, the white halter top with lace edging, hot pink shorts, and finally, the pink polka-dotted flip-flops that show off my "passion pink" toenail polish. It's one of my favorite summer outfits.

"Sure," I tell him. "I'm happy to be your assistant today."

He smirks. "How about you just keep me company? I'd hate for you to get grease on an outfit like that." Whistling under his breath he makes another full body scan.

"I could always slip it off before we get to work?"

"If you slip it off now, no work gets done. Later today I plan on removing every inch of your clothing." He steps closer and I feel the heat radiating off his body. "...slowly, one piece at a time, finally rewarding all my hard work with the sight of your naked body."

The last few words are whispered so softly I barely hear

them, but all of my senses register their meaning. Involuntarily my body shudders and I nod in complete approval of his plan. Slipping my hands behind his neck, I pull his face down to meet mine and kiss him with all the passion and heat of a woman in desperate need. His arms enclose me and he hauls me up tight against his body, letting me feel how his need matches my own.

I pull back slightly and smile up at him. "So...that bike of yours?"

"What bike?" he groans into my mouth before kissing me again. Eventually, we need to come up for air and between pants, he finally agrees that it's time to quit giving the neighborhood a free show.

In the garage, he grabs a five-gallon bucket, flips it, and places his jacket over it. "Your throne, Princess."

He's called me Princess before, usually to accuse me of being spoiled, but today it sounds like an endearment and I smile at him before taking the offered seat. "Thanks."

Kyle has my full and undivided attention. I'm fascinated as he assesses the damage to the bike, with a heavy scowl, and then rolls a battered, red tool chest on casters near his work area. He'd told me he found some replacement mirrors earlier this morning from a local guy he knows that buys, trades, and sells vintage motorcycles and parts so he starts by removing the damaged ones.

"Luckily this tank is a single wall," he tells me as if I'd actually understand.

"Oh well, thank goodness for that!" I laugh and he looks over at me with a raised eyebrow and sexy smirk.

"New bikes have double walls but the thinner, single walls on older bikes makes it easier to pop dents out," he explains.

"That makes sense, I guess. Can you do it?"

"Have some faith."

"I have complete faith in you," I tell him seriously.

He frowns slightly, but it doesn't last long. Turning back to the bike, he runs his hand along the large dent a couple of times and then walks over to a long, homemade workbench running the length of the garage. He plugs in a long, black cord and comes back with what looks like a hairdryer and an aerosol can with a thin, red straw protruding from the nozzle.

"Is that a hairdryer?" It's banged up and flecked with several different colors of paint but still recognizable.

"Yeah. This won't fix it completely, but it's a good start. I've already drained the tank, so this shouldn't take too long."

He spends the next several minutes blasting heated air at the highest setting over the dent. Next, he grabs the aerosol can, telling me it's compressed air. When he sprays it over the heated tank, I can see a layer of frost start to spread and the indentation starting to pop forward slightly.

"Wow. That's amazing."

"It's just a little science," he shrugs.

"It looks a lot better."

He's still frowning. "Not good enough."

Reaching into the tool chest, he extracts a long screwdriver and starts winding layer upon layer of black electrical tape over the flat end. He then pokes it down into the tank, applying pressure to the dent from the backside. Again, this lessens the amount of damage. When he grabs a large hammer with a wooden handle and tube of superglue, I'm stumped. The screwdriver trick made sense. I have no idea what he plans on doing now.

He opens the glue's cap and squeezes a large dollop of the clear goo to the flat bottom of the hammer's handle and then glues it directly into the center of the dent.

"Ummm... Kyle?" I ask, confused. "Why are you gluing a hammer to your bike?"

He grins. "Watch."

After letting the glue set, he grabs the head of the hammer with both hands. I see the muscles in his arms flexing and straining the limit of his T-shirt's sleeves as he braces his feet and jerks back with one swift motion. The hammer pulls free, Kyle barely catching himself before falling, and there is an audible pop as the majority of the dent disappears. The downside is this process also removes a large section of the paint.

"Will it be hard to fix that?" I ask. If I get a single chip in my nail polish, I remove it all and start over. I imagine it would be even more noticeable if he tries patching the paint on such a large area.

"The paint doesn't matter. I've got one more trick up my sleeve for this dent and then I'll sand down the whole tank, fill any places I can fix with Bondo, and then shoot the whole thing fresh. I worked too hard to make it perfect to have her looking half-assed now."

I'm beginning to realize Kyle doesn't "half-ass" anything.

Removing a blood pressure cuff from a box under his workbench, he starts rolling it tightly and stuffing into the tank. It takes some maneuvering but eventually he gets it all the way in and he starts pumping the bulb to inflate the cuff.

"Where did you get one of those? Have an ex-girlfriend that was a nurse?" I can't help teasing him.

"Well, now that you mention it..." he grins. "There might have been a nurse or two. There was also a doctor, a flight attendant, a real estate agent, and oh... the gymnast..."

I cross my arms and glare. "Shut up, Kyle."

"Yes, ma'am." He winks at me and I roll my eyes. He thinks he is so funny. "I got the blood pressure cuff for eight bucks on ebay, Kinleigh. Believe it or not, I haven't had that many ex-girlfriends."

"Just one night stands?" *I shouldn't have said that.* What he did in the past has nothing to do with me.

"I'd be lying if I said I haven't had a few, but it's not as bad as you think. Regardless of my reputation, I do have some restraint in my personal life."

"Good to know."

Kyle shakes his head, probably hoping I drop the subject. I take pity on him and sit back to watch in silence again. After continuing to inflate the cuff a little longer, we both hear the dent make another pop, a little louder than it had when the hammer technique had done its job. Now the bike has only a shallow indentation and Kyle looks pleased with his efforts.

The rest of the afternoon is spent on the prep work for the new paint. Kyle tells me he has a friend with an auto-body shop that will let him use it after hours to do the shoot and then it will be as good as new.

Afternoon has turned to evening and he pulls a long string attached to a bare bulb in the middle of the garage to give him enough light to clean up his tools.

"Can I help with anything?" I ask, feeling useless.

"I got it," he assures me. "Almost done." He pulls the wad of tape off the end of the screwdriver, slips it back into the tool chest drawer, and then looks around to make sure everything is in order.

"You're very handy, Kyle." I look at his grease-stained, capable hands and imagine them getting to work on me later tonight.

"I had to be."

I look up, startled by his serious tone. "I guess you had to be the man of the house? Since your dad left?"

Grabbing a rag from a hook on the side of the workbench, he furiously scrubs at his hands and avoids my gaze. "Yeah, something like that."

"You are a great son and it is very obvious your mom appreciates all that you have done for her."

"I know she does. She worried about me a lot when I was growing up. She worked hard and did her best, but she married my dad when she was very young and didn't have any real job skills. She ended up having to take any crap job she could get to make sure the bills were paid after he ran out on us. I always felt like it was my job to fix everything and keep our old junk running as long as possible. I did yard work because she didn't have time and I didn't want her to be embarrassed by our house. I made good grades, even though my friends laughed at me for studying so much, so I could go to college and be able to take care of her. Then I screwed everything up and didn't finish school and..."

I walk over and lay my head on his shoulder. "What happened?"

He stiffens. "It doesn't matter. I worked it out. It took longer than it should have, but eventually I got my GED and then my business degree. I'm saving everything I can. One day I'll work for myself and make sure my mom never has to work again."

"I told you, I have faith in you. I believe you," I assure him. He relaxes under the surety of my belief.

Clearing his throat, he steps back a little and looks down at me. "Hungry?"

"Starving!"

He throws the rag into an empty bucket and beckons me to follow him into the house. In the small mudroom that looks to be an addition to the home, he steps out of his scuffed motorcycle boots and peels off his socks. This sight of his bare feet below the tattered hem of his jeans does weird, fluttery things to my stomach. I know there shouldn't be anything provocative about a guy kicking off his shoes, but it feels strangely intimate. *Why? For heaven's sake, he's seen me in flip-flops and barefooted on numerous occasions.*

"Kinleigh?"

"Huh?" I force my gaze back to his face.

"I was just saying that Mom knew we would be here today and she left a casserole in the fridge. All we have to do is warm it up."

"Your mom is awesome." I lick my lips in anticipation of her comforting, homemade food and the possibility of seeing even more of Kyle.

"Agreed."

In the kitchen, he pulls a large jar from the cabinet underneath the sink. Unscrewing the lid, he reaches in and comes away with a hand full of something thick and creamy, reminding me of the shortening I put in my homemade buttercream icing.

"What is that?" The smell is weird, with a chemical undertone.

"It's GOJO," he tells me.

That was no help at all. "It's what?"

He laughs at my ignorance. "It's a hand cleaner. It has a gritty pumice in it and grease cutters. Mechanics use it to clean their hands."

"Oh. Alright. If you say so."

"I say so. Would you mind pulling out the casserole?" He scrubs his hands and forearms thoroughly with the cleaner, paying close attention to his nails.

"Sure." I open the door to the ancient white refrigerator. It's the type with rounded edges and a shiny silver handle that you pull forward to release the door's catch. Inside I see a yellow baking dish with small orange flowers decorating the sides. I gently lift the glass lid to peer in at a combination of noodles, chicken, tomatoes, and a cheesy sauce. My stomach grumbles loud enough to make Kyle laugh.

Ignoring his amusement, I scoop a large portion onto a plate and pop it into the microwave. Four and a half minutes later, I divide half of the steaming meal onto a second plate and set them both on the table. In the meantime, Kyle has finished cleaning up, grabbed a couple of forks, and popped the tops off a couple of beers.

"Ewww..." I turn up my nose at the bottle he offers me.

"What?"

"I don't like beer."

Shaking his head in disbelief, he grabs a can of soda for me. "Your dad owns a bar, you're dating a bartender, and you hate beer?"

Brightening at his words, I can't help but ask, "So...I'm dating a bartender? As in, exclusively dating a bartender?"

He slowly lowers himself into the chair across the table from me and throws a scowl my way that would rival my dad's. I'm sure his intention had been to reprimand my flippancy, but all I feel is encouraged.

"Kinleigh... I don't share. You're mine. Only mine." He takes a deep breath, waits a second, and finishes with a question. "That good with you?"

Pure joy washes over me. "Only if that means that you're mine and I don't have to share you with anyone else either."

His hand steals across the table and our fingers lace together. "Agreed."

Nothing has ever sounded sweeter. Kyle is frustrating and

stubborn. He drives me crazy most of the time. He's also kind and generous, makes my heart find new rhythms to sing, and sends my body into a state of hyper-awareness that leaves me raw and unsettled. He is exactly everything I want and there is nowhere I'd rather than be than sitting across from him, at his mom's kitchen table, sharing dinner and finally being honest about our feelings for each other.

As expected, the meal is delicious and disappears faster than good manners dictate, but I refuse to be embarrassed. I was hungry, the food was great, and who decided girls shouldn't have normal appetites?

"My mom will be happy you enjoyed dinner so much," Kyle says with a sexy smirk and raised eyebrow as he glances at the one, lone noodle stuck to my plate's edge.

"If I'd grown up with DeAnna as my mom, I'd have to live in sweatpants," I admit. "My mom is more of the 'know every take-out menu' kind of cook."

"Really?" He looks surprised. "You love to bake so much, I assumed your mom was amazing in the kitchen."

I laugh. "No. Like yours, my mom was a single parent and after school, I would go home with my friend, Summer. I spent many weekends there too. It was like my second home. Summer's mom was always baking something from scratch and she taught us both everything."

"She was a good teacher. I can't imagine anyone baking better cupcakes than you."

I warm from his compliment. "Thank you."

"So…" He gets up and takes both of our plates to the sink before turning back to me and wrinkling his nose. "I'm overdue for a shower."

Standing up, I walk around him until I can press against his back and reach my hands around him. My fingertips skim over the hard ridges of his abdomen and I turn my face enough to press my cheek against the back of his neck, relishing the heat of our contact.

"Okay. Let's take care of that," I whisper softly and the immediate tension in his shoulder blades assures me I have his attention.

Unhooking my hands, he spins to face me. "You sure?" His voice drops low and betrays a skeptical hopefulness that pulls at my heart.

Placing my hands on either side of his face, feeling the sharp-edged planes of his cheeks and the light stubble along his jaw, I nod my head. He releases a loud breath I hadn't been aware he was holding. Without another word, he pulls me down the hallway and into a bathroom situated between the only two bedrooms in the house.

Earlier he'd given me the grand tour, plus I'd needed a couple of bathroom breaks today for obvious reasons and to touch up my lip gloss, so the room is familiar. With white floor tiles, pale green walls, and a modernized, walk-in shower, the room is old-fashioned but functional. And, just like the rest of the house, it is immaculately clean.

Grinning at me like a mischievous little boy, he grasps the bottom edge of his black T-shirt and tugs it over his head. I hear myself exhaling too loudly when I catch sight of his perfectly sculpted torso. *No one should look this good. It's no wonder women throw themselves at him.* I want to say something. I want to explain how beautiful he is and what he does to me... but my thoughts are a jumbled mess and not a single coherent thought presents itself.

"Were you planning on observation only?" he asks, slyly.

"Oh!" I look down at my still fully clothed body. "No. No, I want to join you."

He cocks an eyebrow. "Good."

Taking his cue, I kick my flip flops into the corner of the room and untie my halter top. It joins my discarded shoes right before I shimmy out of the little pink shorts. Knowing half-naked women throw themselves at him daily at work is a little hard on the self-esteem, but when I see his eyes run hungrily over me, all doubt melts away.

"You are flawless," he breathes out and his words send tingles along my now flushed skin. *This is finally going to happen.*

Reveling in the confidence, I now feel, I close the distance between us. My fingers easily pop the button of his jeans and then slowly slide the zipper down, enjoying the sight of his chest rising and falling rapidly in reaction.

"So are you," I assure him.

When I grab the denim riding low on his hips, it only takes one quick tug for them fall to the floor. He deftly steps out of them and reaches behind me to unhook my bra.

"Do all of your bras and panties match?" He whispers as he nuzzles into my neck, right below my ear.

Looking down at the pale green satin with pink stripes, I grin. "Definitely." I let the bra fall forward and he swallows hard when my breasts are fully exposed. The last barrier is a quick and simple fix. Held by thin ribbons on each hip, they only require the simplest pull for the bows to disappear, but his forceful yank has probably ruined the poor panties. I couldn't care less.

I'm momentarily startled when he starts the shower and a powerful jet of water crashes down, echoing over the tiled room. Soon steam is swirling around us and I'm lost in the feel of his work-roughened hands caressing every inch of my skin.

"Come here." There is a husky quality to his voice that I've never heard before and my body responds to it. My bones have become liquid and flames are threatening to consume me from the inside out.

He yanks the elastic tie at the end of my braid and slides his fingers into my hair, untangling the strands. Tipping my head back, I close my eyes and luxuriate in the heaven of his fingers kneading against my scalp.

My fingertips dance along the width of his broad back and trace the ridges of his shoulder blades before seeking out each knob of his spine, from top to bottom. When my hands travel farther south, I realize his boxer briefs had pulled a disappearing act. I don't miss them. Good riddance.

Intertwining our hands, he pulls me into the shower with him. The sting of the hot water pounding on my chest and stomach while the heat of his kisses assault my back and shoulders from behind is overwhelming. Taking turns, we use the lightly scented soap to slickly glide our hands everywhere and then rotate under the shower's head to rinse.

I don't want to think about my past, about the few guys that I dated and cared for enough to be intimate with. It feels wrong to make comparisons, but I can't help it. They were nice and gentle and I enjoyed the experiences. This is wild abandon and insatiable need coexisting with a tenderness that makes me ache with happiness.

"I want you so much," he purrs after we've rinsed away all traces of the day spent out in the garage. "I want you so much, it terrifies me."

His confession seals his fate. *He's stuck with me now.*

"I believe you, Kyle."

"Oh, yeah?"

Turning to face him, I lower my gaze and grin. "I can see exactly how much you want me."

Hoarse laughter escapes the back of his throat as he presses against me, ruining my view but giving me the gift of feeling his desire. "Kinleigh... I could take you right this second. I could slam into you and finally be where I've only dreamed of being... but I'm really trying to take my time. I want you to want this as much as I do."

"I already do," I admit. "And we have all night. I'm not going anywhere... so whatever fun things you have in mind that we don't catch on the first go 'round... we can make up for on the next."

He groans into my hair. "Hell, yeah."

I feel the light touch of his calloused hands circling my breasts, running down my stomach and thighs, and eventually coming to rest firmly on my backside. Now I'm the one groaning.

"Hold that thought," he whispers into my ear before nibbling at the lobe. "I'll be right back."

"What?" I grunt out in shock. "You're leaving me in here?"

He just laughs in response and slips out of the shower. When I realize what he is grabbing out of his jeans pocket, I relax, glad he is prepared.

Once he is back where he belongs, pressed against me, I wrap my arms tightly around his neck. I'm not cool with the idea of him escaping again, even briefly. He uses this to his advantage... actually, *our* advantage... and grabbing hold of the back of my thighs, he lifts me up until I can wrap my legs around him. Locking my ankles, I shift to help him track the right course.

"You sure, Princess?" His voice is ragged as he strains to wait for my consent.

"I'm not a princess. I won't break or change my mind. Now,

Kyle. Now!"

I'm rewarded with that bad boy smirk that I love right before he presses my back against the tiled wall of the shower and pushes into me with one hard, quick slam. Instinct takes over and I meet every thrust with equal force. Sooner than I believed possible, I feel the telltale tightening that precedes release. When the waves of it hit me, I don't know whether to scream out in pleasure or cry tears of joy. I think I do both and it spurs Kyle into the last frantic movements he needs to meet me.

"Oh my God," I whisper as the water, now starting to lose its heat, continues to beat against us.

"I couldn't agree more," he answers.

We slide down together, a wet, soapy tangle of loose limbs and full hearts.

Chapter Twenty: Kyle
Second Chances

"What the hell are you grinning about?"

I smile even wider. "I'm just happy to be at work."

Ronan's scowl deepens. "Is there any particular reason you're happy to be at work today, Kyle?" Even forced through clenched teeth, every word is clear and well enunciated.

My eyes, going rogue, dart across the crowded bar until I catch sight of Kinleigh. Without missing a beat, Ronan steps to his left and blocks my view.

Does he know?

"I'm just..." *Shit. What do I say?* I can't exactly admit I had sex with his daughter. My grin widens. If I want to be accurate... twice last night and once this morning.

"Just shut the hell up and get back to work," Ronan cuts into my reminiscing before heading off to his office, allowing me the opportunity to stare at Kinleigh again.

This morning I'd woken up, shivering and naked, against what amounted to a body burrito. Kinleigh is a cover thief. When I tried to unroll her from the layers of the quilt, blanket, and sheets... she had responded by curling up even tighter, puckering her face into an adorable pout, and grouchily telling me to leave her alone. If I hadn't been so fascinated by the sunlight streaming in, turning her hair into a palette of gold and corn silk... or the way her dark lashes fanned out on her flushed cheeks... or even the way her two tiny freckles on her jaw are so close they touch at the bottom to almost form a heart... I might have pushed her off the bed and reclaimed my blankets.

Instead, I gently peeled each layer back until one full, perfect breast was exposed. It was irresistible, so it wasn't my fault I had to kiss its rosy peak until she was happy to allow me full access.

Shit. Work isn't the right place to be reliving this. I must have a death wish. Turning away, I get busy prepping the bar for tonight.

Madison slides in a CD, a demo from a local band we will be debuting tonight, and the heavy, thumping beat helps us all pick up the pace. I slide a clean towel along the length of the scarred, wooden bar top and watch as our three regular waitresses, along with Kinleigh, sway their hips and dance around the tables. Their joy is contagious and I feel a familiar tension coiling deep in my core when Kinleigh closes her eyes and starts pushing her hips back and forth in a rhythm that mimics the song and the beating of my heart. How in the hell am I going to be able to wait for our shift to end before having her again? I will never get enough of her.

Without warning, the song abruptly stops and the silence feels louder than the music had been. With perfect, unintentional synchronization, we all look to the stereo. Ronan is standing

151

there with one hand on the knob, one hand extending the bar's cordless phone, and a dazed look on his face that erases his usual frown lines.

Kinleigh is the only one brave enough to step forward. "Dad? You okay?"

"Here. The phone." He pushes it in her direction. "For you."

She hesitates. "Who is it?"

"Mom." Ronan clears his throat. "It's your mom. Amber. She wants to talk to you. You didn't answer your cell, so she called the bar."

Kinleigh smiles broadly and finally takes the proffered phone. "Hey, Mom!" Her voice is sugar and sunlight. Again, I remember last night and how her sweet words had been more like heavy, thick caramel with a touch of something spicy.

Damn. Her cupcake obsession must be rubbing off on me. Since when do I compare women to food?

"I'm sorry. I think my phone is still on vibrate and we had music playing in the bar while we were getting ready for tonight so I didn't realize you were calling."

Everyone else, including Ronan, has gone back to work, but I stand near her, rubbing small circles across her back and shoulders. She smiles up at me and leans closer.

A small chuckle escapes her. "What did you say to Dad?"

I'd like to know what his ex-wife had said to Ronan too.

"You should really come for a visit..." Kinleigh winks at me conspiratorially. "Then you guys could talk in person..."

Kinleigh suddenly straightens up and pulls away slightly.

"Oh... Uh, actually I don't know anything about that, Mom." There is a long pause. "Sure. Yeah, I'll do that."

I look into her eyes and try to communicate my question and concern, but she avoids my gaze. *What's going on?*

"Okay. Bye. Love you too." Kinleigh hangs up the call and tries to muster a smile, but it never reaches her eyes.

"What's wrong, babe?" *I hate seeing her upset.*

"Nothing. There's nothing wrong. Everything is fine."

Why is she lying?

"Kinleigh... talk to me." She doesn't respond well to demands.

"There's nothing to talk about," she stubbornly insists. "Let's just get back to work before the customers start rolling in." She walks away, nibbling on the edge of her lip, with a deep furrow across her normally smooth forehead.

I want to follow her but don't think I should. Our relationship is new and I'm not sure of my footing yet. After my ridiculous attempts to push her away, I'm damn lucky she's given me another chance.

Chapter Twenty-One: Kinleigh
Spill It!

"Madison, can I talk to you?" I lean against the pool table, mindlessly rolling the eight ball around on the faded, green felt.

"Sure." She stuffs her lipstick and a pen into the back pocket of her jeans and turns my way. "What's up?"

Should I tell her my concerns? It's probably just my overactive imagination... and I'll sound conceited.

"Never mind. It's fine. It's nothing." I sink the black ball into the closest pocket.

"Kinleigh." She places one hand on my shoulder and squeezes lightly. "Tell me."

Taking a deep breath, knowing I have to get someone else's opinion, I relent. "Okay. Remember Jeremy?"

"Of course. Tall, blonde cutie you were going out with... before Kyle grew a brain and realized he was mad for you."

I laugh. Madison is great for adding a little lightness to any situation. "Yeah, him."

"What about him?" she asks, narrowing her eyes slightly with suspicion. "Do you have feelings for him? Have you changed your mind about Kyle?"

"No!" I yell out, loud enough for the subject in question to turn in our direction and frown. I smile and wave, trying to convince him that all is well, and I'm relieved when Kyle goes back to work.

"Okay, good... because I think you two are great together. In fact, if I were a betting woman, I'd put money down on my favorite bartender and a certain boss's daughter getting busy very recently."

"Madison!" I feel the blush crawling up my neck and face.

She grabs both of my shoulders and shakes me lightly. "Spill it! Was it incredible? It was incredible, right?" She looks over her shoulder to Kyle. "I love my boyfriend. I love my boyfriend. I love my boyfriend." She grins at me. "I really do love Mike so you won't get any competition from me... but damn, girl... your man is beyond hot and looks like he knows exactly what to do."

My grin has become a full-on smile of epic proportions. "I can't even describe it," I sigh.

"Well you better try!" she insists and I laugh.

"Look, we both know he's beautiful and his body is all chiseled muscles and rock hard perfection..."

Madison groans softly. "Agreed! Go on."

"I love looking at him. I love touching him and running my fingers over his... well, over every inch of him," I explain.

"No doubt!"

"And he knows where to touch me and how much pressure I need and just what to do and..." I pause, not wanting to give out any specific details. It would be a betrayal of what we shared.

"But it's more. Kyle knows how to make my body feel pleasure and I'm in awe of the responses he can pull from me but more importantly, he does something to my soul." I close my eyes and think of how it had felt for him to be a part of me. "I love how smart he is and how he can fix anything. I love how he takes care of his mom. I love how he is protective of me but allows me space to be myself. I love..." I stop, unsure how to put into words all the small things about Kyle that fascinate me.

"You love him," she tells me. "You love Kyle."

"I do. I love him."

"And he loves you." She sounds so sure of this. I pray she's right. "I'm so happy for you, Kinleigh. You deserve this."

"Thanks." I smile at her, glad to have found someone so incredible to be my friend. I left some great friends back home when I'd moved here to work for my dad and I miss them terribly but having Madison around is making my transition much easier.

"So, the reason you wanted to talk to me? Was it just to gloat about your hot night of sex? Because Mike has been out of town all week for a business conference and I'm so damn horny right now, it's embarrassing and I'd appreciate it if you don't rub it in that your man is close enough to jump daily!" She's laughing, but her words remind me of the reason I'd sought her out.

"No, it's not about Kyle. I want to talk to you about Jeremy."

Madison frowns lightly. "What about Jeremy?"

"We had fun, but he's not Kyle. I didn't want to string him along or give him false hopes, so I immediately let him know after Kyle and I talked and worked things out, that we didn't have a future. I hoped we could remain friends at least."

"That's the right thing to do," she assures me.

"But he didn't take it so well."

Looking at me anxiously, she sits down on a chair at the nearest table to wait for my explanation. "What do you mean?"

"He just sounded disappointed at first but then he made some nasty comments about Kyle. I was mad but tried to blow it off and chalk it up to a little jealousy..." I flush again, concerned she'll think I have an overinflated opinion of myself. "...but then he starts blowing up my phone with constant texts and calls. I've quit answering, but he leaves these long voicemails about what a mistake I'm making and how he deserves another shot."

"Wow..." She wrinkles her nose in disgust. "I feel sorry for him, unreciprocated feelings suck, but desperation is not a good look for anyone."

"I have to keep my phone on silent all the time now because I worry that either Kyle will think I'm still encouraging Jeremy, or even worse, get pissed at him and decide to intervene."

"So you don't get off to the idea of two hot guys battling it out for you?" she teases.

"Absolutely not."

She nods. "I agree. But what more can you do? You've told him it's over so hopefully he'll get tired of trying and just move on."

"I hoped that too but then the other day I ran into him at the grocery store. He played it off like a coincidence, but it kind of creeped me out." I shudder lightly.

Madison stands back up and slides close enough to bump our shoulders together. "Everyone has to buy food occasionally. Try not to read too much into it. It's just an unfortunate, random occurrence."

"Maybe... but then my mom just called and..."

She stands up straighter, paying close attention. "What does your mom have to do with Jeremy?"

"It's probably nothing... but she told me that a bouquet of

tulips was delivered to her house this morning and there was a card. It said, 'Thank you for raising the woman of my dreams." She assumed it was from Kyle, I've told her we are together now, but I don't think so. He's very thoughtful, but he's never met my mom and I can't see him putting that out there while this is still so new. Plus, Jeremy always brought me tulips, never roses or carnations or anything. Just tulips. What do you think?"

She takes a minute to think about my question. "It doesn't sound like Kyle to me either. Maybe if the card said he was looking forward to meeting her one day, I could think he was really trying to make a good impression but if that was the case, why wouldn't he sign it?"

I run my hands up my face to cover my eyes, feeling a headache threatening. "I know. A part of me wants to just ask him, but again… if it isn't him, what would he think?"

"And you think it's Jeremy?"

"I shouldn't assume, but it's the only explanation I can think of." *Please let it just be a silly mistake. Maybe the florist just mixed up the address?*

"Okay, well we don't know anything for sure. Give it a few days and maybe an answer will present itself. In the meantime, be careful," she begs.

"I will. I promise. Thanks for listening. I know it sounds ridiculous, but I just needed to talk about it. I'm sure everything will be fine." I put on a brave smile and take a deep breath. "Let's get back to work!"

"Okay." Madison turns to leave but hesitates and looks back to me. "I almost forgot… Remember my extra apron you borrowed when you helped me wait tables last week? Can I get that back? I only have two and I ripped one of the pockets on this one and I'm afraid I'll forget and lose someone's change or something. I would have fixed it, but I can't sew for shit."

I wince with embarrassment. "Of course! Oh my God, I'm so sorry I forgot about it. Let me run upstairs and grab it for you. Dad said he is about to order some new ones for everyone, but I should have given it back sooner."

"No problem!" she assures me. "I appreciated the help. We were packed that night."

I go into the storeroom and jog up the metal stairs that lead to my apartment's hallway. The darkness that awaits me at the final step surprises me. There is a large, industrial light fixture hanging in the middle of the hall that never goes off. My dad insists on it for safety. Walking to the end of the hall, where the metal door leading to the outside staircase, I flick the light switch up and down a couple of times and realize the bulb must be out. I know it was on when I'd come in from my night with Kyle earlier today so it had to have happened very recently. There is enough ambient light coming from the staircase and the one small window high above the exterior door to make out the door to my apartment so without worry, I make a mental note to mention the bulb to Dad. Reaching into my pocket, I realize I don't have my keys.

I groan in frustration. *Where did I leave them?* I know I had the keys when I came home or I couldn't have gotten into the apartment. Did I leave them on the coffee table? That's where I usually drop them. I distinctly remember locking the door as I left to go downstairs to the bar, but I do that by pushing the button on the door's handle from inside before pulling the door closed behind me. The key isn't needed to lock up except when I add the deadbolt above the knob. Dad is always after me to remember that extra step, but I'll admit I forget regularly. *Had I done it today?*

"He's going to kill me," I mutter to myself, dreading the lecture I'm about to get from dad. I have no choice but go back downstairs and get the extra key from his office.

As predicted, he isn't happy.

"Damn it, Kinleigh!"

"I know. I'm so sorry. I thought I put them in my pocket before I came down," I insist... again.

He hands me the key from his top desk drawer. "Don't lose this one or I'm going to have to call a locksmith."

"I won't. I'm just going to pop upstairs and get my set and I'll put this right back where it goes."

Crossing his thick arms over his chest and glaring, he sighs to emphasize how hard it is to parent such an irresponsible child. "Don't let that boy put your head in the clouds. Think. Make good choices. Be safe."

On tiptoes, I give his rough cheek a quick peck. "Yes, Daddy. I love you."

He just grunts and pushes me toward the door.

Chapter Twenty-Two: Kinleigh
Head In The Clouds

"How the hell do you work in those shoes? How do women even walk in them, come to think about it?"

I laugh at his question. "You get used to it," I insist, looking down at my eyelet lace espadrilles with a four-inch wedge heel and satin ribbon tied around my ankle. "Because they're adorable."

Kyle leans close, his mouth so close to mine I can feel his warm breath sliding across my lips. "You are adorable, Princess."

"Ohhh," I breathe out, waiting for him to lean that last quarter of an inch, to feel the silky heat of his kiss and the gentle rasp of his skin against mine.

"Kinleigh?" And with that one word from Brooke, the spell is broken. The waitress comes into the storeroom looking for me.

"I'm over here," I tell her, from behind the metal shelves that fill half of the room, trying not to let my frustration show.

"Oh…" She spies Kyle and me in the darkened corner. "Sorry to interrupt."

She doesn't look sorry, I think to myself. "What do you need, Brooke?" I grumble.

"Ronan needs last week's beer invoice. He said he thought you had it?"

I sigh. I do have it. I'm working on a new budget and the file folder is in my Victoria Secret tote bag that I took to Kyle's house yesterday but never brought in from my car. "Tell him I'll go grab it."

She winks at me. "Will do. I wouldn't take too long, though. I don't blame you, of course," she pauses to look Kyle up and down, "but you probably don't want your dad to be the one to discover you in here next time."

"Thanks, Brooke."

She takes one last look at us before sashaying herself back to the bar.

"Okay, you go grab the file, I'll make sure the bar is in order…" Kyle smirks. "…and we will pick this up where we left off. Deal?"

I throw my arms around his neck and lean my forehead against his. "Deal."

Walking into the cool night air, glad for the large pools of yellow light cast by the security lights in our back parking lot, I hum the melody of the song that had been playing in the bar during cleanup. It was an upbeat piece about finding exactly what you hadn't realized you were missing. The lyrics play over in my head and I smile, agreeing with the sentiment.

When I get to the trunk of my car, I remember I still don't have my keys. I'd used Dad's spare to get into my apartment, but my key ring hadn't been on the coffee table as I'd expected. I have no idea where it is. If I don't find them soon, I'm going to have to ask my mom to overnight the extra set of car keys and have dad make a copy of his apartment key.

Maybe Dad had a point about my head being in the clouds lately.

Walking around to the driver's side, hoping I'd left it unlocked and could at least use the button under the dash to pop the trunk, I stop suddenly when I hear the crunch of footsteps behind me.

"Who's there?" I ask, whipping around to scan the few cars still in the lot. I can't see anyone but I'm nervous and my senses are on full alert. I strain my ears and swear I pick up the sound of soft breathing. "Kyle? Is that you?"

I know it isn't Kyle. He would never try to scare me like this. And I am scared. I back away from the darkness beyond the light's reach, taking one last good look before preparing to sprint for the safety of the back door.

Almost convinced it's my imagination I start to turn. That's when I hear him.

"Kinleigh. We need to talk."

Turning slowly toward the voice, I see the silhouette of a tall man between me and my escape. Even with the backlighting making it impossible to see his features, I recognize him.

"What do you want, Jeremy." Trying to sound confident, I'm betrayed by the slight quiver at the end.

"Don't be scared. I'd never hurt you." He takes several long strides and now he's close enough for me see his expression. It doesn't match the assurances he's given me. He looks mad.

I want to back up, but I'm afraid to leave the safety of the light. If someone comes looking for me, I'd be hard to spot in the dark areas of the parking lot.

"I need to get back inside. We can talk later."

He comes even closer. "But you never answer my calls."

I start to stammer. "I will. I wi-will answer. I promise. I'll call you tom-tomorrow."

With one last step, he's right in front of me. "No. I don't believe you. We can talk right now."

He reaches an arm out in my direction and I jerk away, finding my back pressed against my car. "Don't touch me, Jeremy."

His lips become a thin line of hate. "You were fine with my touch before that fucking bartender got hold of you."

Mentioning Kyle bolsters my confidence. I will not cower in front of this creep. I haven't done anything wrong. I press my finger against his chest, tamping down my revulsion at even this contact with him.

"Look, I'm sorry if I hurt your feelings. I felt bad about it, but your actions since have ruined whatever sympathy I had. Leave me the hell alone!"

"Sympathy?" His laugh is bitter and cold. "I don't want your fucking sympathy." He grabs both of my shoulders and shakes me hard enough to rattle my teeth. "You are going to wake up one day and realize you let the best thing in your life slip away because of mistakenly believing that unworthy piece of shit actually cares for you." The back of my head slams against my car's window. "He just wants to sleep with you! Don't you see that? He will use you and throw you away. I was so patient. I was taking my time because I really believed you would be worth it! I thought you were different!"

My vision is going dark around the edges and there is a wet heat tickling along my scalp when Jeremy suddenly releases me and I slide down to the gravel. I vaguely register yelling. It sounds like Kyle.

Chapter Twenty-Three: Kyle
You Have The Right

A blinding fury consumes me. I've only felt this kind of rage one other time and the consequences had been devastating, but I can't stop.

"Get your fucking hands off her!" I reach out, ripping him away from Kinleigh and see her crumple to the gravel near her car. A part of me wants to run to her, scoop her up and make sure she is okay. A bigger part of me wants to kill the son of a bitch that dared to touch her.

"She deserves better than you!" he screams at me. He has a point, but she sure as hell doesn't deserve someone like him.

I've known his type. They will go to any lengths to get what they want, regardless of who gets hurt. Anyone that thinks violence against a woman has justification should be reserved a special place in hell.

"Kyle?" Kinleigh's voice is a whisper and I see her put a hand to the back of her head and come away with fingers coated in her own blood. Then her eyes roll up, the lids come down, and she passes out.

My hands clench, I pull back and slam a fist into his face. There is a satisfying crunch with the contact and he falls to the ground, bringing his arms up to protect his face.

"Go ahead, you piece of shit. Beg me to stop!" I threaten. He just laughs.

"I don't beg for anything," he spits out. "And soon Kinleigh will be the one begging. She'll realize I'm the right man for her and she'll beg me all night long."

I know better. I know not to let his ridiculous delusions affect me but the thought of him still pursuing her has my blood boiling. He needs to know it is in his best interest to stay far away from the woman I love.

Grabbing the front of his shirt, I pull him up and let my fist make my point. Once I get started, I can't stop. I keep seeing him as he slammed Kinleigh into her car. I see her blood spilled across her fingers. I see him laughing at me, convinced he has the right to ever touch her again. I disappear into the black hole of my fury.

It seems like hours and it seems like only seconds when I feel myself being pulled off him. Several strong arms shove me to the ground and a knee presses into my back as they bind my hands behind me. What must be a plastic zip tie digs into the flesh of my wrists and I register flashing blue and red lights making a strange dance of shadows along the back wall of the bar.

"Kyle Taylor, you are under arrest." A uniformed police officer jerks me up and forces me into the back seat of his cruiser. "You have the right to remain silent. Anything you say can and will used against you in a court of law. You have the right to an attorney. If you cannot afford an attorney, one will be provided for you.

"Kinleigh!" I strain to see her, but my line of vision is limited now that I'm inside the car.

"Kyle! Oh my God! Kyle!" she screams with panic. Hearing her voice calms me down considerably. At least I know she has regained consciousness. Seeing her eyes flutter shut when she collapsed on the pavement had almost killed me.

"I'm fine!" I yell in her direction.

"Ma'am! Stop! You need medical attention!" an unfamiliar voice calls out through the chaos.

I see Kinleigh has escaped the paramedics and is running toward me. She slams her palm against the glass of the window as a cop tries to pry her away.

"Ma'am, step away from the vehicle."

She ignores him. "Kyle! We will fix this." She's crying and her shoulders shake with the sobs. "Nothing is going to happen to you! I promise."

I smile at her naivety. I've been through this before. I have no illusions. "Just go see the doctor, babe. I'm fine."

Ronan has walked over and he wraps his arms around Kinleigh's waist to pull her back.

"Take care of her!" I yell at him as the officer in the driver's seat finally puts the car into gear and starts to pull away.

Ronan has no expression, but I take comfort in his nod of acknowledgment.

Chapter Twenty-Four: Kinleigh
A Matter Of Public Record

"This isn't his fault! You can't arrest him!" I insist for the hundredth time as I slam my fist down on the desk, causing a stack of papers in a plastic tray to flutter. "He was saving me."

"I hear what you're saying ma'am." The officer has dark hair graying at the temples and a weary expression that says he's seen and heard it all.

"Then why did you arrest him?" My head aches and my sinuses are so swollen from crying that it's almost impossible to breathe. My tears are all gone now, though. I'm just mad... angrier than I've ever been in my life.

"Miss Walters, I've already explained this to you." Placing his elbows on his desk, he steeples his fingers and sighs. "Mr. Taylor might have had good intentions, but he did more than just pull Jeremy Duncan off of you. He beat him unconscious. The man is in the hospital."

I close my eyes, trying to drown out the noises of the precinct. When Dad and I had arrived, we'd been escorted past a prostitute arguing about entrapment, a sullen teenager being lectured by his parents for spray painting a local monument, and a rail-thin man so strung out he literally couldn't sit still. This place is a freak show. Kyle doesn't belong here.

I try again. "Officer Bradshaw..."

"It's Detective Bradshaw, ma'am."

I clench my teeth and smile, refusing to get sidetracked. I don't care what his rank is. I just want answers. "Look, I'm sorry that Kyle took it a little too far but..."

"A little too far?" my dad cuts in. "Honey, I like Kyle, you know I do but..."

"Dad, you aren't helping," I whisper, but he interrupts me again.

"Kinleigh, I'm glad Kyle showed up when he did. I want you to press charges against Jeremy and get a restraining order. I'd have hit him too if I'd seen him push you but... did you see him when Kyle was done? His face was a bloody mess. Kyle got out of hand and I'd like to think it was the heat of the moment and you're safe with him but..."

"I AM safe with him! You know him, Dad. Kyle doesn't have a temper or a history of violence! He was protecting me!"

Bradshaw clears his throat loudly. "Actually ma'am, Kyle Taylor does have a history. It's a matter of public record."

I go still. This can't be happening.

"Kyle has a police record?" I slump in the chair, aware of a ringing in my head and the slamming of my heart.

"What did he do?" my dad asks. I see his hands clench the wooden arms of his chair tight enough for the skin over his knuckles to stretch smooth and white.

"He assaulted a man, put him in a coma and he almost died."

I draw in a breath and feel faint, unable for several seconds to release it. "No," I say in desperation. "He would never..."

My Kyle? My gentle Kyle that takes care of his mom's house, helps me babysit and takes me on romantic picnics?

I remember back to our picnic and how mad he got at the silly kids that caught us making out. Their taunts had made him spring up, ready to fight.

"It is in his favor that he was coming to your aid," the officer tells me, "but considering it is his second assault charge..."

The obvious implication hangs in the air.

"Can I talk to him?" I ask even though I have no idea what I'd say to him now.

"Not yet. He's still being processed. He'll be arraigned in the morning and his bail set. It's probably best if you go home."

I continue to sit in the hard chair, in the middle of the police station, trying to figure out how to deal with all of this.

"Kinleigh," my dad takes my arm and pulls me up with him. "Let's go. The doctor told you to rest."

I nod woodenly and allow him to guide me out of the station and into his car. He starts the engine but doesn't back out of the space.

"I'm sorry, baby." His voice is soft, but it fills the silence between us and makes me cringe.

"I know what the cop said," I croak out, not recognizing my own voice. "But we have to ask Kyle the truth. We don't know the circumstances. He's a good man."

My dad sighs and I see the pain in his eyes too. He cares for Kyle and I'm not the only one reeling from this news.

"We'll talk to him. I promise to hear his explanation."

I lay my head over on his strong shoulder, thankful for the

support he's always given me. "Thank you."

"You just need to understand we may not like what we learn."

"Nothing will change how I feel for him, Dad."

"Maybe not," he concedes. "But caring about him isn't enough. You can love someone and know they aren't right for you and your life. I should know."

"You mean Mom?" I ask.

"I'm sorry. You don't need to hear that right now."

"No, I want to know. You loved each other, I remember that. Why didn't it work out?"

He leans his head back against the seat rest and takes a deep breath. "I did love her. I still do and probably always will. We tried Kinleigh. We wanted it to work for your sake and for our own, but my assignments were classified and dangerous. My military career was important to me and I was proud of what I was doing for my country. When I was able to come home, I needed a safe place to land. Amber is a good woman and she tried, but the secrets were killing her. I couldn't tell her where I'd been or what I'd been doing. She was home alone, raising you and making a life I was mostly absent from. She resented my silences and I got tired of feeling like a stranger. We made the decision together to separate to make sure our love didn't become hatred."

"I'm sorry, Dad. She still loves you too, you know. She's tried dating a few different men, but it never works out. They're never you."

He smiles at me with a tenderness he usually hides. "She's the most amazing woman I've ever known, but she was smart to let me go. She deserves better. Learn from us, honey. Move on. You don't need to worry about Kyle's temper and what he's capable of doing when he's angry."

"It's not that easy. And I think you were wrong to end things with Mom too. You aren't in the military anymore and there's no need for secrets. Why don't you try again?" I put my hand over his where it rests on the gear shift.

He raises both our hands and places a quick kiss on my knuckles. "It's too late."

"I don't believe that, Dad. I don't believe it's too late for either one of us. I have to have faith that Kyle can explain what happened."

Chapter Twenty-Five: Kyle

Pain

"Kyle Taylor, you've made bail."

"What?" I look up from the cot as the police officer removes a ring a keys and unlocks my cell. He doesn't even look old enough to be in college, with an irritated, acne-covered face and dark, greasy hair combed back from his forehead.

"Someone posted bail and you're free to go," he tells me. "You can get your belongings and the information about your hearing on your way out."

"Who?"

"Do you want out of here or not?" he asks with impatience. "I don't know who did it, just be thankful."

Giving up on getting anything useful out of the young officer that's let the power of his position give him an inflated sense of self-worth, I follow him down the corridor and up a flight of stairs to the main room of the station. He directs me to a long counter near the exit.

I collect my wallet, keys, and cell phone and turn to see Ronan waiting for me.

"Did you do this?" I ask.

"Yeah." He looks as uncomfortable as I feel.

"Thank you," I whisper, my shame making it hard to say more.

"Uh-huh," he grunts, equally unsure what to say about the situation I've put us in.

"How's Kinleigh?" I have no right to ask, but I have to know she's alright. I've spent every minute of lockup worrying about her.

"She'll be fine."

"What did the doctor say? Does she have a concussion?"

"No. She didn't hit her head too hard luckily, but the edge of the window trim got her just right to make a small laceration. Head wounds bleed a lot, but she didn't even need stitches."

I say a small prayer of thanks. "I'm glad."

Ronan frowns. "Let's get out of here. We need to talk."

I nod my head in agreement. There's no sense in putting this off. "Okay."

The ride back to the bar is silent. I feel his questions building a wall between us and I know my refusal to answer some of them won't be good.

Following him into his office, I close the door behind us and sit across from him. Several more minutes pass before he starts. He can't make eye contact and I know he must have learned about my record.

"I can never thank you enough for saving my daughter, Kyle."

"There's no need." I would do anything for Kinleigh.

"Do you even want to know how Jeremy is doing?" His disappointment in me stings more than I thought it would. His approval matters.

"How is he?" I know I went too far, but I'd really believed he meant to really hurt her. Maybe more than she could recover from.

"He's stable. Luckily there's no permanent damage, but he doesn't look too pretty right now."

"Okay." I'm glad I didn't kill him, but I'm not really sorry he's hurt.

"I've had to do some... well, some things more violent than I'd like to admit, in order to keep a lot of people safe. It's a hard thing to live with. If I'd been the one to go out in that parking lot, I can't say I'd have made a different decision either."

I let out the breath I'd been holding, glad he understands. The strain in his eyes lets me know he isn't finished, though.

"If last night had been a unique situation, I'd be in your corner one hundred percent, but..."

"But..." I prompt.

"But, it wasn't unique. You have a criminal record for a past incident where you almost killed a man. I'd like to think I've come to know you over the last several years, Kyle, and I'm trying to understand this. I need you to explain it to me. I want to believe you had no other choice and that you aren't a violent man with an uncontrollable temper."

"I did what I had to do," I tell him, refusing to say more.

"Kyle, that isn't good enough!" An angry red suffuses his face. "I don't want my daughter with someone that could flip a switch one day and hurt her!"

I stand up, furious that he could think I would ever lay a hand on her. "I would die before hurting Kinleigh!"

The heat of his anger fades. "Sit down. I believe you. But I also believe you could hurt someone else and put her through the

175

anguish of watching you pay for it. It would drag her down with you. If you can't explain your past to me, I think it's best if you move on."

I think about what he's saying. I've always known I wasn't good enough for her. He's right. I need to move on.

"Okay," I finally tell him. "I assume you don't need two week's notice. You can just mail my last paycheck."

"Kyle..." Ronan swipes a large hand across his face. It looks like he's aged ten years in the last ten minutes. "Please talk to me."

"There's nothing to say. Thank you for paying my bail. You'll get your money back, I promise." I turn to leave. I love this job. Ronan has been like a father to me. And Kinleigh? She's the most important thing in my life. She's the reason I have to leave.

He starts to follow me. "What am I supposed to tell her?"

"The truth. Tell her, she deserves better. She's the only one that doesn't understand that."

I pass through the bar and walk into the bright afternoon light. Kinleigh's car is still parked in the same spot in the center of the lot. I think I can see small splotches of her blood, now dried into dark stains, on the pavement near the passenger side door.

Looking away, I continue past her car and stop at my motor-cycle. Now back to her former beauty, I remember the day spent in my mom's garage, fixing the Scrambler. I also remember that night of unbelievable passion and acceptance I'd found in Kin-leigh's arms.

I throw my leg over the seat, pull the helmet down over my face, and kick the bike to life. I want to go to my apartment and escape everything that's happened, but I have one more person to disappoint today. I need to talk to my mom. She knows about last time and she needs to know what's happening now, but my gut clenches and roils at how much pain this will bring her.

Why do I always hurt the women that love me?

Chapter Twenty-Six: Kinleigh
Complete And Total Wreck

"Where is he?" I demand after looking around the bar, peeking into the storeroom and my father's office. My dad has the decency to look ashamed.

"He isn't here."

I make a small noise of frustration that's somewhere between a snort and a grunt. "Obviously! Why isn't he here, though? You said you would be picking him up from the station and bringing him to the bar so we could talk. You insisted I wait so you had some time to talk to him first, and I didn't like that plan, but you assured me it would be best. So where is he, Dad?"

"He left."

"Cut it out!" I yell and he flinches.

"Watch the tone, young lady. I'm still your father." His reprimand lacks any anger and that scares me. I've never been able to get away being disrespectful.

"I'm sorry. Please, no more vaguely stating the obvious. Tell me what happened."

He nods his head in defeat. "I talked to him, but he didn't have a lot to say. No answers or explanations. He refused to defend his actions or explain his record. I gave him every chance but…"

"But what?" I ask, fear curdling in my stomach.

"When he couldn't reassure me about his past actions I let him know it was best if he moved on."

I inhale sharply and shards of ice pierce my heart. "You… You fired him?" I whisper with incredulity.

"We both agreed that this was for the best."

I sink to the floor, sitting on the step that leads to the small stage near the back of the bar. *Oh, Kyle. Surely he doesn't think I want him gone?*

"Kinleigh… I know this hurts now but…" My dad tries to put a hand on my shoulder and I jerk away.

"You might have been able to leave my mom because things got tough but I'm not you!" I scream at him. "I believe in doing what's necessary to make it work with the person you love!"

I instantly regret my outburst. My dad doesn't deserve the hateful things I spewed in response to my own feelings of helplessness. He should be furious with me for my lack of respect, but instead, he's heartbroken. Without saying a word, he silently walks into his office and closes the door behind him, leaving me alone, ashamed and scared for my future.

Pulling my knees up, I wrap my arms around them and lay my head over. Two days ago I'd been the happiest woman in the world. Now my world is a complete and total wreck and I'm causing some collateral damage on my own.

I slide my phone out of my pocket and dial Kyle's number. It goes to voicemail. I'm not surprised. My next move is to send him a text, pleading for him to call me. It takes ten minutes of staring at my dark, silent screen before I give up and shove it back into my pocket.

Knowing the employees will begin arriving soon for tonight's shift, and unable to pretend I'm not in pain, I trudge up the stairs and retreat into my apartment. I drop my clothes onto the living room floor, grab a bottle of wine from my refrigerator and head for my bathroom.

Running a bath at a temperature near scalding, I add some scented bubbles and let myself melt into the water. My skin instantly flushes and beads of sweat form along my hairline. It takes several minutes of the heat for my muscles to relax and my jaw to unclench. My next step is to pull the cork from the almost full bottle of Moscato and take several long swallows.

Worry has exhausted me and my eyelids are starting to gain weight with every passing second. My chin slips under the water's surface slightly as the bubbles tickle my jawline and the tip of my nose. I might have drifted off completely if the shrill sound of my cell phone, still in the pocket of my discarded clothing, hadn't jerked me back awake.

Kyle!

Convinced he's finally calling me back, I jump out of the tub and slosh a great wave of the sudsy water onto the floor, soaking my bathmat and not caring. Naked, freezing, and risking damage to the beautifully finished wood floors of my apartment, I run for the phone. Praying I make it before he hangs up, I slip and fall to my knees. Pain sets in.

"Ow!" With one hand pressed against the bruised lump already forming on my left knee, I use the other to grab the leg of my jeans and haul them closer. Desperately fishing the now silent phone from the pocket, I look at the screen.

It hadn't been Kyle calling. The name across my screen sends me into a rage that's almost debilitating. *How dare Jeremy try to contact me after what he's done!*

Pulling the soft, chenille throw blanket from the arm of my couch, I wrap it around me and start to shake violently. What am I going to do? Kyle won't talk to me. The creep that ruined my life is calling me. I've been teased my whole life for being an eternal optimist and the 'glass half full' girl, but now I have no plan and can't find a single silver lining.

I'm scared to look at my phone again when it chimes with a text message a few minutes later. When I do, it's as I feared.

"Kinleigh, I'm sorry for hurting you. It was an accident. Please forgive me," scrolls across the screen under the name Jeremy Duncan.

Is it better to ignore him or tell him to leave me the hell alone?

While I try to decide, another text appears. "I'm in a lot of pain. Come see me. I know your bartender is in some trouble. We should talk this out."

Is he blackmailing me? Is he willing to drop the charges if I agree to see him? Can I afford not to find out?

"I'll come tomorrow," is all I reply before powering off my phone and heading back to the bathroom to grab the bottle of wine.

Chapter Twenty-Seven: Kyle
Selfish

"You know I don't practice criminal law, right?" he reminds me yet again.

"I know," I tell him.

"You'd probably be better off with someone else." This is something else he's repeated several times in the last hour.

"I want you, Logan. I trust you."

Sighing and giving in, he finally opens the folder in front of him. "Okay. I need to know everything."

"I think it's pretty simple. That fucker hurt Kinleigh, so I hurt him."

"Taking that approach won't win you any points with the judge."

"I don't expect any. That courtroom will take one look at me, the bartender with long hair and tattoos, and then take a good look at poor, clean-cut Jeremy's battered face and decide my guilt before I ever open my mouth."

Logan frowns at me. "It's my job to show them the truth. They need to see you're a good man that had to defend his girl-friend against a psychopath."

"Good luck," I throw out before grabbing another beer from the fridge in my cramped kitchen. "Want one?" I ask, tipping the bottle in his direction.

He shakes his head and studies the papers in front of him. "So, we need to talk about your prior conviction."

"Why?" I've tried so hard to bury what happened and now everyone wants me to relive it.

"It will be pursued by the prosecutor to show a history of violence. I need to know everything so I can be prepared to de-fend your actions." He stands up from my table and begins to pace across the linoleum.

I sigh and think back to the conversation I'd had with my mom last night. After a long crying spell, she begged me to tell Kinleigh and my lawyer and anyone that needed to know, the truth about what happened last time. As always, she's willing to bear any pain in order to save me. I reminded her that I swore to never discuss it again or make her relive that horror but still, she kept insisting.

I'm so fucking selfish. I want to tell. I want to explain it all and have Kinleigh understand and forgive me. I want Ronan to look at me again without any disgust and know his daughter is safe with me. But how can I do that when every truth I share is a horror my mom wants to hide? How do I hurt her, even if it saves me?

"Kyle?" Logan prods.

"There isn't much to know. You have the file. I was almost eighteen and I beat the shit out of a guy. He had a broken nose, three fractured ribs, and a concussion that put him in a coma for six days. The judge took into account it was my first offense and my age, plus the guy didn't want to press charges, so I got community service, anger management classes, and probation. I got off light."

"Are we not going to talk about the fact that the guy was your stepdad?" he asks.

"Irrelevant," I insist.

"I find that hard to believe."

I jump up to throw the empty bottle into the trash and grab another. "Believe it."

Logan takes the new beer out of my hand and grips my shoulder. "Kyle, I know you. I trust you. Help me, help you."

I swallow hard, unable to meet his gaze. "He hurt my mom," I whisper.

"That's what I figured," he says softly. "Please tell me."

"He hurt her bad, Logan. It just kept getting worse and I didn't know what else to do to save her." I close my eyes, replaying that horrible day in my head. "And then, when I saw Jeremy smash Kinleigh's head against her car the other night... I couldn't help it. Once again a man was trying to hurt a woman I love. I planned on hitting him once, just to get him off of her... but he kept taunting me, saying horrible things, and I just..." I sink to the floor of my kitchen and close my eyes.

"Okay. I get it. We'll make them see what happened and why. I won't let you go down for this, Kyle."

I nod my head, thankful for Logan's support, but doubtful it will make any difference.

After two hours of rehashing every awful detail from my past, and explaining everything that had happened a few nights ago at the bar, Logan stands up and stretches. He's probably tired, but my exhaustion stems from making new bruises over old scars. I'm not proud of some of the things I had to do but as usual, I was the only one there to take care of it. I'll pay any price to make sure my mom and Kinleigh are safe.

He grabs his coat off the back of the chair. "We have a good chance, Kyle. Don't give up. In your same position, I might have done the same thing. The thought of anyone hurting Charli... Jaci..." Logan closes his eyes and balls his fist. "God, Kyle... I'd probably kill someone that laid a hand on them in violence."

Clapping a hand on his shoulder, I nod my agreement. I believe him. He understands. "Thanks for coming over. I swear I'll find a way to pay you for this."

"Don't be ridiculous. We're friends... and let's be honest, if I didn't help you, my wife would make my existence a living hell," he says with a serious face and a twinkle in his eyes.

I laugh, for what feels like the first time in forever. "Well, regardless of your sense of self-preservation... I do appreciate it."

"If I were helping you out with something else, I would say 'anytime' but..."

"Yeah, let's hope this is the only time."

He shakes my hand, promises to call me tomorrow with an update, and leaves. I wander between my small kitchen and the barely larger living room of my apartment. With too much pent up frustration, I'm at a loss to find anything meaningful to do. I'm currently unemployed, for the first time in my life. My mentor, former boss, and friend thinks I'm too dangerous to be around his daughter and is disappointed in me enough to keep his distance. My new girlfriend, the woman I love, is better off without me and therefore being strictly avoided.

What in the hell do I do now?

Chapter Twenty-Eight: Kinleigh
Desperate Times, Desperate Measures

"Kinleigh?"

Waking up to pounding on my door, starts an even fiercer pounding in my head. It's an unpleasant sensation I recommend avoiding.

"Kinleigh?" Another bang.

Ow.

"Kinleigh, open up. It's Madison."

I groan, realizing she isn't going away. "I'm coming," I croak out.

"What?" she yells behind the door.

"Oh, God..." I hold both sides of my head as I get up, desperate to regain some quiet. I have to endure four more knocks before I shuffle far enough to open the door.

"Oh..." Madison looks at my uncombed hair, pink robe with a cupcake embroidered on one lapel and a dark wine stain on the other, and my single striped knee sock before wrinkling her nose in disgust.

She obviously doesn't approve of my current appearance, but my biggest concern is what happened to my other sock. *I know I started out with a matched pair.*

"Hi," I offer half-heartedly.

"You look like shit, sweetie," she responds in the kindest of tones.

I snort. "Thanks."

"Can I come in?"

Opening the door wider, I step back and allow her to enter. She takes two steps and then folds me into a tight hug. I hug her back.

"Oh, Kinleigh... I'm so sorry."

"I'll be fine," I assure her. Last night had been bad. After I'd finished off the bottle of Moscato, I'd thrown my robe over my oldest pair of sweatpants and snuck downstairs to snag another bottle from the bar. In my hurry, I'd accidentally grabbed a bottle of Merlot, hoping to not get caught. I'm not a big fan of reds and ordinarily wouldn't have touched the stuff but... desperate time and desperate measure and all that garbage.

Madison pulls me over and onto the couch next to her. "Are you sure?"

"Yep," I reply with conviction. I'm not the type to wallow long. I had a good cry, drank too much wine, and now I'm done. "My dad let Kyle go. He won't return any of my calls and I'm worried we won't get past this. But what more can I do? I've tried to tell him thank you for saving me. I want him to know I understand and I'm not upset. I want him to explain what happened when he was younger and how the gentle, kind man I know could be brought to do such a thing. I want to listen to him and be there for him, but I can't do any of that if he won't let me."

"So, what now?"

"I'm hurting. I love him, Madison. I've done what I can and now it's up to him." I've thought a lot over the last several hours. I love Kyle, truly and completely, but I can't be that girl that curls up in a ball and ruins her life because a man was too stupid to let her love him. I hope he comes around, but I won't sit and wait for it.

"He loves you too. I know it." She stresses her belief by squeezing my hand.

I smile at her. "I think so, too."

"Okay, then maybe..."

Madison is interrupted by my phone ringing and skittering across the coffee table. Involuntarily I flinch, worrying it might be Jeremy again. Thankfully, I see it's my mom. I hadn't called her, but I'd bet my future cupcake business that my dad had.

"I need to take this," I apologize as I answer the phone. "Hi, Mom."

"Oh, baby... How are you?" Her concern almost makes me forget my promise to myself and I start crying again.

"I'm doing okay. Promise," I try to assure her. Madison stands up and waves as she leaves me alone to talk to my mother.

"You don't sound fine. Have you been drinking?"

How do moms always know?

"Nope," I tell her, but the accompanying hiccup probably doesn't help my case.

"Hmph. Just promise me you aren't driving anywhere today? Don't make me call Ronan and tell him to come take away your keys!"

"Mom," I say patiently. "I'm not drunk and I'm not going anywhere, so leave Dad out of it."

She sighs heavily into the phone. "Well, he sounds almost as bad as you. He really likes that boy, doesn't he?"

"Yes, ma'am. We both do." Poor Dad. Kyle hurt him when he hadn't trusted him and then I made it worse with my anger at him.

"Maybe you could use some new scenery?"

"What?" Does my mom think I should take a vacation while the man I love goes to trial for almost killing the jerk that attacked me?

"Come home, baby."

Home? Is Mom's house even my home anymore? This apartment has become my home. I like working at the bar. I like my new friends and I've built a life. And Kyle is here. This is home. "I don't know. I appreciate the offer, but…"

"I don't mean for forever, Kinleigh. I just mean for a visit. Come hang out with me. We will get facials, manicures and maybe even a massage. You can even see Summer while you are here. She and her son are in town to visit her parents and you girls haven't caught up face to face since high school."

It's tempting. "Okay. That sounds good, Mom. Kyle isn't ready to talk yet and maybe a few days away will help. I'll drive up in the morning if that's okay, and will be there by lunch?"

"Great! I can't wait to see you and…" her voice falters slightly, "tell your father hello for me."

I grin unexpectedly. "Sure thing. Bye, Mom. I love you."

"I love you too. See you tomorrow."

Hanging up, I'm surprised to realize I actually feel a little better. I miss my mom and hopefully a few days away will make Kyle understand he needs to let me in. Taking a whiff of the collar on my pink robe, and recoiling in disgust, I stand up with renewed purpose. First on the agenda is a nice hot shower and then on to whipping my hair back into shape. I've never been a fan of those messy 'this isn't important to me' styles. I'm also a planner and highly organized, so I'll go ahead and pack my suitcase and get everything laid out for my trip. Lastly, I'm going to apologize again to my dad for the awful things I said and fill him in on my plans.

As I turn around to get my life back on track, my phone goes off. "Come see me," the screen taunts. "We have things to discuss."

Chapter Twenty-Nine: Kinleigh

Prostitution

"You don't know how much it means to me that you came."

Why hadn't I noticed earlier how slick and slimy his voice is? How had I fallen for his nice guy routine?

"Make it quick, Jeremy. Say what you want to say so I can leave."

His hospital room has a recliner in one corner and rolling stool near the bed, but I opt to stand in the doorway. It sickens me to look at him. It would be awful to see anyone that had suffered a violent assault but even with his face a swollen canvas of bruises, the hardest part is watching his battered mouth form a gloating smirk of victory. He's enjoying this.

"Kinleigh, we have a lot to discuss and I want to take my time and make sure we cover all the bases. Please come in." He raises one arm, dangling IV tubes and palm up, and beckons me in.

I pinch my lips tighter in a futile effort to control my anger and shake my head in refusal.

"Well, this isn't a very good start to our negotiations, now is it?" Suddenly, without warning he drops the act, his voice going brittle and hard. "Sit down, Kinleigh!"

Afraid for Kyle's future, I reluctantly do as he asks.

He smiles. "Now, isn't that better?"

"Please," I beg quietly, "just tell me what you want."

His smile widens. "I've been telling you what I want from the very beginning. You just haven't been listening. You let that..." His face becomes an ugly sneer, "*bartender*... convince you to be with him." He has to take a deep breath before continuing. "Women are all alike. A man works hard to provide her with everything she could possibly need and showers her with affection and kindness. And what does she do? She leaves him for a guy that treats her like dirt."

I'm getting the distinct impression he isn't talking about just me. Someone had screwed him over and he can't forget it. His bottled up rage and sick need to twist what happened between us is making me nervous.

"Jeremy, I never..."

"Sh-h-h." He puts his finger over the cut that bisects the middle of his lips. "I'm talking now."

As hard as it is, I close my mouth and look directly into his ice blue eyes.

"You know, when we went on our first date, I thought it went really well." He smiles in remembrance and my stomach curdles. "I let you go on and on about your family and your plans for your future. I was encouraging and attentive. I made sure to keep eye contact and used non-threatening physical contact at regular intervals."

It sounds like a calculated list to convince a woman you are a decent guy and not a psychopath. Hearing his calm explanation has my heart's rhythm beating double time. What I had seen as a relaxed evening out had actually been a well-executed plan to lower my guard.

He continues, unaware of my anxiety. "I wanted to get you alone so badly. I knew if I could get you home, you'd see how great we could be together. But I thought you were one of the good ones, a keeper, and wouldn't go that fast. So, in deference to you, I chose a well-lit and well populated, public place. I didn't try to push you. I wanted you to come to me when you were ready, so I continued to take you out to nice places. I brought you flowers and held your hand. A couple of kisses at the end of the night seemed appropriate, so I let myself have that little indulgence. I did all of this for you!"

I swallow hard. "Jeremy... I did like you. I did have fun..." *Does he notice my use of past tense?* I certainly don't like him now.

"I know!" He sits up straighter in the bed and winces in pain. "I went over everything you said in our texts and phone conversations. And I watched you at work when it was busy enough I could hide in a crowd and you even seemed happy when you were out running errands. I made you happy, Kinleigh!"

Oh my God. I feel faint. He's been watching me.

"And then..." His lips form an ugly sneer. "The bartender decides he wants you."

"It wasn't like that," I protest.

"Yes, Kinleigh it was. You are kidding yourself if you think differently." He talks to me patiently, like I'm a confused child. "He doesn't respect women. He whores around with whatever slut catches his attention at the bar and just uses them and moves on to the next one. I know his type. I saw you lusting after him and it made me sick. But I forgave you. You're just young still and don't realize how men like him operate. When he hurt you and you waited on my table that night, I knew I could save you."

"Save me?" I whisper in disbelief and fear.

"I wanted to show you the way things could and should be. You needed to be in a good relationship with a man that would worship you. My mom left when I was young because she had her head turned by an asshole just like that bartender. My dad told me every day of my life what a whore she was for chasing after some creep that showed her a few tricks in the bedroom. He was right, but I also knew he hadn't been a good husband. I decided then that when I found the right woman, I would make her my everything so she'd never leave."

"Jeremy! We barely know each other! We went on a couple of dates and you decided I was your forever?" My voice is escalating and I can't reign it in. I feel like I've entered another dimension and normal rules don't apply. I need to leave.

My loud panic doesn't even give him pause. "Oh, Kinleigh. I knew from almost the first moment I saw you. I had truly hoped you would come to the same conclusion on your own, but I can see it might require a little more to convince you."

"Convince me? Convince me of what? I'm convinced that Kyle was right and you are crazy and need to be stopped!"

"I'm not crazy!" he spits out with the first honest reaction I've seen since arriving. "Let me explain how this is going to unfold. I'm not kidnapping you or forcing you to love me! I know that you just need time to see things clearly. I'm not being unreasonable. All you have to do is drop the charges against me, they won't stick anyway since it was an accident, and agree to spend time with me."

"What?" I ask incredulously. He can't be serious.

"You tell Kyle it was all a misunderstanding and agree to go out with me for the next several months. I'll drop the charges against him, as a gift so you know I'm sincere about this working out."

"You want me to prostitute myself?" I raise a single eyebrow in disbelief.

"No!" he responds with disgust. "I'm not expecting you to sleep with me until you want to of course. I just want us to be together so you come to feel the same for me as I do for you."

"Let me get this straight..." I stand up and walk over to his bed, placing a hand on the railing. "You will make sure the assault charges against Kyle disappear and all I have to do is drop my charges against you and date you?"

"Exactly!" he beams with pleasure, believing I finally understand and will agree.

I smile. "Never."

Without a backward glance, I leave the hospital room with its bank of monitors, smell of disinfectant and its absolutely insane patient.

Chapter Thirty: Kinleigh
Guilt

"Think this rain will ever stop?" Mom asks for the third time, with her forehead pressed against the glass of the French door leading to her backyard.

My drive here started out fine, but by the time I was an hour or so from arriving the storm had started. Sheets of rain pounded against the windshield, almost rendering my wipers useless. I'd even turned off the radio to ensure no distractions while I concentrated on seeing the lines of my lane and monitoring the drivers around for me for any loss of control. The stormy ride in had been scary. Now, safely tucked on Mom's couch in my pajamas, wrapped in the crochet blanket my Gran made for my parents as a wedding gift, I feel safe. It is a blessing I fully appreciate.

"Oh!"

I grin over the rim of my mug of hot chocolate when a bolt of lightning streaks across the sky. The accompanying thunder rattles the door's panes enough to startle my mom. After all, she was the one who taught me the boom follows the flash of light.

"Mom, please sit down. Sprinkles is freaking out." The poor little dog hiding under the foot of my blanket is now shaking hard enough for ripples to migrate along the surface of my cocoa.

This finally brings her away from the outdoor light show. "My poor itty baby girl..." She scoops the quaking dog from under my feet and nestles the ball of fur under her chin. "Mommy won't let that mean old storm get you!"

My dad had bought Sprinkles for me when I turned sixteen. I wanted a little puppy to dress up, carry around and be my side-kick. At that age, we are selfish enough to think everything is an accessory to our life... and I might have also been obsessed with Legally Blonde. Things don't always go according to plan, though. Realizing that puppies need a lot of effort to potty train, plus the fact they might not want to ride around in giant purses, had come as a shock. With me at school for most of the day, my Sprinkles had soon become my mom's Sprinkles.

"Before this weather hit, I was hoping we could lay out by the pool today while we catch up. Then maybe tonight we could enjoy a nice dinner at the new restaurant that opened over by the school. I've heard good things. Tomorrow could be a spa day and then we could make some time for you to see Summer or some of your other friends. I think there's a new romantic comedy play-ing too that we could try to squeeze in and then..."

"Mom," I interrupt with a laugh. "I've missed you too, but I really think I'd like this trip to be a bit more low-key if that's okay?"

"Sorry, baby. I just thought if we did some fun things, it would take your mind off of... Well, you know, everything."

Looking down into my mug, I think about 'everything.' The

more I think about things, the more I feel I am to blame. Kyle had pegged Jeremy from the start and hadn't trusted him. If I hadn't agreed to that first date, hadn't encouraged him, we wouldn't be in this mess.

"Kinleigh Nicole Walters, you stop that right now," my mom demands.

"What do you mean? I'm not doing anything." I try to keep my voice from trembling.

"I know my daughter. This is not your fault."

Tears swell and I swallow hard to hold them back. "Really? I'm not so sure. I don't blame myself for Kyle acting stubborn and giving up on us... that's on him. But what about Jeremy? I'm the one that let him into our lives."

"You did what anyone would do. You accepted a date with a handsome young man that seemed kind and genuine. You had no way of knowing he has issues. His horrible behavior and Kyle's extreme reaction to it, are not your fault. I also know that you and your dad had words over Kyle."

Shame burns in my cheeks. "Oh, Mom I should have never talked to Dad like that!"

"He understands. You love that boy, and Ronan may not like that his daughter is a grown woman with a love life, but nothing you could say or do will change his feelings for you. Your Daddy loved you from the minute we found out I was pregnant." Now my mom is the one holding back tears. "He would lay down at night, holding his hand over my belly, and tell you how loved and wanted you were. He swore to move heaven and earth to make sure no one ever hurt you or stood in the way of your dreams. The reason this is so difficult for him now is because he feels like he failed you."

"What?" I sit up abruptly and set my sloshing mug on the

end table. "He's always been there for me!"

"I know that. You know that. But Ronan? Well, he sees it as his failure because his baby girl, living and working in *his* building, was physically assaulted while under his care. And, instead of him being the one to save you, Kyle did. Anyone else being your protector would be hard for your dad, but for it to be Kyle? He considers Kyle almost as a son and now with him facing serious charges, Ronan feels like he failed him too."

"Oh, Mom..." I never gave much thought to the fact that my father would blame himself. It made me want to pick up the phone and apologize again.

"Ronan is a strong man, the strongest I know..." Her eyes take on a faraway look I've only ever seen when she talks about Dad. "He will find a way to fix this. You'll see."

Suddenly, something very curious occurs to me. "Mom, how do you know all of this?"

Her eyes sharpen and dart away. "Know what?"

"How Dad feels? And all the details of what happened? We haven't really talked about it yet."

Now she is blushing. "Oh, that. Well... Ronan... I mean... your dad called me to fill me in on everything the night it happened, naturally!" She sets Sprinkles down and moves over to adjust the collection of frames that line the fireplace mantel.

"I knew that, but how would you know about Kyle's refusing to tell us about his past? That was a couple of days later."

"Hmmm?" Picking up my almost empty mug, she moves to take it into the kitchen.

"Mom!" I jump off the couch to block her. "Are you and Dad talking?"

"We've always talked about the things that concern you." She tries to go around me. "You are our daughter."

I start grinning. "Oh, my God! You are. You and Dad are *talking*! Not just about me but really *talking!*"

She forces a frown, but I can tell she wants to smile. "Mind your own business, honey," she chirps in a singsong voice before managing to outmaneuver me.

Chapter Thirty-One: Kinleigh
Payment

Grabbing for my phone, my heart seizes when the screen shows it's from a blocked number. "Hello?" I hear my own hesitation.

"Kinleigh?"

The feminine voice on the other end is familiar, but I can't place it. "Yes. This is Kinleigh."

"Hi, dear." There is a long pause. "This is DeAnna."

"DeAnna?" My temporary relief from learning it isn't Jeremy contacting me is replaced by panic. What's happened to warrant this unexpected call? Can I take any more bad news?

"Yes, Deanna Taylor... Kyle's mom?"

"Yes, ma'am! I know who you are. Is everything okay? Did something happen to Kyle?" I sit up in bed and start fumbling for the digital clock on the bedside table.

"He's fine! I'm sorry, I didn't mean to worry you."

My heart slows a bit and I fall back onto my pillow. It's still early, only eight o'clock. Between the stresses of driving below the speed limit through heavy rain, the booming thunderstorm and trying to maintain a calm appearance through the emotional chaos that has overtaken my life the last few days, I must have crashed when I came upstairs to read after dinner. There is something soothing about the familiarity of being back in the room where I'd had tea parties with my dolls, confided my secret crushes to my friends during sleepovers, and cried myself to sleep when my high school boyfriend told me we should see other people.

Rubbing the sleep from my eyes, I stifle a yawn. "It's okay. It's nice to hear from you," I assure her. I really like DeAnna and I got the impression she likes me too.

"I'm sorry to call this late. Actually, I'm sorry to call and bother you at all."

"You are not a bother!" I insist.

"Thank you. That's very sweet of you to say."

"Did Kyle ask you to call?" It doesn't seem likely, but I can't think how she would have my number or why she would need to talk to me.

"No!" The sudden volume of her response startles me. "He has no idea I'm calling. He would be so mad at me!"

This bothers me. A lot. *Why would he care if his mom calls me?*

"I actually did a bad thing to get your number..." She laughs softly.

Now I'm curious. "What did you do?" I can't imagine DeAnna doing anything truly bad.

She laughs again. "Well, I asked Kyle to come over. I told him I needed him to fix the sink drain again but really I just needed to set him straight on a few things." I smile at her tone. "We ended up not seeing eye to eye. He can be rather stubborn at times."

"Really?" I'm sure she can tell how NOT surprised I am to hear this characterization assigned to her son.

"So," she continues as though I hadn't added anything, "When he went to the bathroom, he left his phone on the table. He's never been very imaginative with his security password. He normally uses his birthday, even though I've told him that is dangerous."

I grin in the dark, picturing his tiny, dark-haired mother peeking down the hallway as she slides her hand across the table to snatch up his phone and punch in his password. "And you used it to get my number?' I guess.

"Well, I knew if I asked him for it, he would have told me to stay out of his business!" Her firm justification for the sneaky maneuver doesn't surprise me. I've seen my own mother act the same way when she feels she is doing something for my own good.

DeAnna continues, "So I did what I had to do so I could contact you."

"I'm happy to talk to you, of course, but what was so urgent? Do you need me for something?"

"I need you to help my son see reason!"

I rub the bridge of my nose with my thumb and index finger and take a deep breath. I may have to ask my mom for some aspirin. The last few days have given me more headaches than I usually have in a year. Trying to get Kyle to see reason might end up being the biggest headache of my life.

"I tried," I tell her. "He won't return my calls."

"So you're giving up on him?" I hear the challenge in her tone.

"I didn't say that. I'm still hopeful that we will get past this. I have to believe that with time, Kyle will explain why he has pulled away from me. I do know he saved me from Jeremy. At first, I was grateful but still shocked that he..." I don't want to admit to Kyle's mother that he'd scared me when I saw what he'd done to Jeremy. "Well, I guess... I had a hard time understanding why Kyle took it so far..."

"And now?" she asks.

"It still seems excessive but..." My talk with Jeremy at the hospital replays in my head and I shudder. "I've decided that a milder warning would have been useless." *Should I tell her that even Kyle's extreme warning hadn't done much good?* Jeremy is still trying to see me, after all.

"Kinleigh, Kyle doesn't want you to know the details of last time."

"I know that. And I want to trust him. I *do* trust him. I have to believe the man I love would never hurt another human being without just cause."

"Oh..." escapes in a long breath. "You do love him, don't you?" she asks, almost pleads.

"I do." It's simple and it's the truth.

"Well, then to hell with what he wants!"

My shock takes a moment to register. "Excuse me? What do you mean, DeAnna?"

"He doesn't want me to tell you about Gary, but you need to know and understand."

I feel guilty for the excitement her words bring. Kyle won't be happy, but I may finally know the truth. "Gary? Is that the other man he..."

DeAnna takes a deep breath before launching into her story. "Yes. Gary was my husband, and Kyle's stepfather."

Leaning into my phone, afraid to miss a single word, I wait silently and pray she continues.

"Gary wasn't so bad at first. He worked for a local shipping company, we met when he was making the deliveries to the office where I was temping at the summer Kyle turned fifteen." There is a short pause. "He was nice to me and I'd been single so long. After Kyle's father left us, I was too busy raising my son to worry about dating. Like all moms, there comes a time when your child doesn't need you as much. Kyle was gone a lot with school, work and his friends... Well, Gary could be very charming and I was taken in. I was a fool."

"Don't say that." I sympathize with her story. Hadn't I been nursing a broken heart and not a small amount of hurt pride when Jeremy had fooled me?

"I think I wanted to believe he was a good man, so I over-looked the small signs. No one is perfect and I rationalized that it would be good for Kyle to have a man in the house. We could use the help with the bills and chores too. Those aren't very good reasons to marry someone, but it made sense to me then."

I thought about how hard it must have been for DeAnna, try-ing to do everything alone. I can't imagine marrying anyone for any reason other than true love, but who knows how differently I might feel if I was in her situation. If you think something is best for your child, I'll bet you could do almost anything.

"What happened?" I asked sure the story is about to take a turn for the worse.

"It was okay for a little while. Kyle didn't really like Gary, but he didn't dislike him either. Or maybe he just hid his feelings to make things easier for me. It wouldn't surprise me. He's been known to do that."

I'm betting that is exactly what happened. After all, he saw through Jeremy.

"The real turning point was when Gary got hurt. Kyle still did most of the work around the house, but I kept begging Gary to clean out the gutters. They were clogged and useless, and Kyle was busy studying for upcoming finals. Our ladder was old, Gary had a few beers in him, and the neighbor's dog had managed to dig his way under the fence into our yard. It was a bad combination. The fall shattered his knee. He couldn't work and lost his job. Once he was on disability, he spent all day drinking away those checks."

My Mom peeked her head into my door to check on me, but I waved her away. I had to know it all.

"Gary blamed me. My bad ladder, my insistence he clean the gutters, my very existence had caused all his bad luck. The first time he hit me, I was almost convinced I deserved it."

Grabbing my pillow from behind, me, I clutch it to my chest and squeeze my eyes shut, willing the tears to wait. I can't let DeAnna hear me cry. If she can hold it together, she deserves me doing the same.

"Gary wasn't stupid. He made sure my bruises could be easily hidden, and never on my face. He knew how Kyle would react. Even though Kyle wasn't a full grown man yet, he was strong and tough... and fearless. Eventually, though, Kyle noticed me moving slower and losing interest in everything. He suspected the cause. He grilled and harassed me constantly to tell him the truth, but I denied it all. I was so ashamed."

"It wasn't your fault," I tell her.

She continues as though I hadn't spoken. "Then... that night... I came home and..." A quiet sob rips through my phone and makes my heart break for her.

"You don't have to tell me," I whisper.

"Yes. I do. You need to understand. If Kyle had come home and found Gary hitting me, he would have been furious. He would have probably punched him and made me leave. But when Kyle's shift ended early and he showed up two hours before he was expected and saw what Gary was doing to me... trying to make me do..."

I'd wanted to know the truth, but now I'm scared to death of what I'm going to discover.

"Gary's drinking was bad enough but toward the end, he'd also started gambling. He played poker with some friends and liked to go to the track, but he really loved sports and betting on all the games. Apparently, his debt was getting out of hand and no one was willing to let it float any longer. One particularly nasty man came by our house a lot. I never liked him. He always made me feel dirty just by looking at me. Gary owed him the most money and they made a deal to clear that debt. I was the payment."

A sick acid burns in my stomach and threatens to come up. I want to get in my car and drive all the way to DeAnna's house and tell her in person how sorry I am. No one deserves to suffer that sort of humiliation.

"Did he... Did Kyle get there in time?" I ask, fearing the answer.

"Yes. Gary had me pinned down and the creepy bookie was laughing and ripping at my dress and..."

"Oh, God." She must have been so scared.

"Then my Kyle came home. The creep ran, but Gary wasn't fast enough. His knee was still pretty useless. I've never seen my son like that. Gary is lucky he isn't dead."

"But why was Kyle prosecuted?" I'm practically yelling now in frustration. "He was saving you!"

"I know. I was an emotional wreck and traumatized. I was completely broken and unable to speak. By the time I'd healed enough to realize what had happened, Kyle was going to trial. I wanted to testify and tell the jury everything that happened and why Kyle had gone berserk but he wouldn't let me!"

"Why?" My poor Kyle. *How had he dealt with so much while so young?*

"He was protecting me, of course. He had the public defender because we couldn't afford a good lawyer. Gary was claiming I was cheating on him with that awful bookie. The bookie was backing up the story too. Kyle's lawyer said it would be hard to prove otherwise, and I would have to tell my story over and over to try and convince a jury that I was innocent. Everyone would know our business, and bring more shame to our family. He said that Kyle should accept a deal. So he did."

My breathing has turned into deep, desperate draws of air that leave me unsatisfied and gasping. Tears burn as they flow down my cheeks. I want to tear down the world and remake it into a place that would never let something like this happen.

My voice is no longer my own. Gone is the playful lilt and childish ignorance. It's deep, hoarse and a raspy shadow of itself. "And now?" I ask. "He still won't talk about it?"

"I think I convinced him to tell Logan. He is a good friend and a good lawyer. He'll help Kyle."

"But why didn't he tell me?" I beg, needing to know why he didn't trust me with the truth.

"He's ashamed. He thinks he should have known what was really going on earlier in my marriage and that he failed me. He believes you will think of him as a failure too."

"I don't!" I yell into the phone, ignoring the searing pain that burns through my throat. "He saved you. He saved me."

DeAnna makes a noise of satisfaction. "I knew you would understand. Go to him, Kinleigh. Help him. Please."

I'm already jumping up and pulling my suitcase from under the bed. By the time I hang up with Deanna, I have my clothes packed and I'm looking for my mom so I can say goodbye and head to Kyle. I have to see him and now is not soon enough.

Chapter Thirty-Two: Kyle
Forgiveness

"Thank you for coming. Have a seat." Ronan indicates the barstool next to his. The bar is closed tonight and we have the place to ourselves.

"I'm good standing," I tell him.

"Sit down, Kyle," he insists and as usual, I comply.

"I said you could just mail my check. There's no reason for us to talk again."

Ronan slides a half full glass of a dark amber liquid in my direction and I notice he has an identical one if front of him. "I disagree."

I sigh and take a drink, enjoying the smooth burn as it slides down my throat. He'd pulled out the good stuff.

"I'm sorry, Kyle."

My head jerks up and I stare at him in shock. "What?"

"I'm sorry. I don't want you to quit. I..." He gulps half of his glass and sets it back down a little too hard. "I was wrong. I panicked."

"You weren't wrong!" I insist. "Kinleigh is lucky to have a father like you, someone that always wants the best for her. You are right to keep us apart."

"No. I'm not. You are a good man and you've proven that time and time again. I've known you for years, practically watching you grow into an adult before my eyes, and you've never been quick-tempered or violent. I don't know what happened all those years ago, but I know you now. I know you walked out that back door and..." He pauses and takes a deep breath. "You saved my daughter. You protected my baby girl and I repaid you by not trusting that you were doing what had to be done."

I'm stunned. "Ronan..."

"Can you ever forgive me?" He looks me directly in the eyes. There is no anger or fear, just remorse.

"There is nothing to forgive," I assure him.

"I disagree."

I lay my head down on the bar and close my eyes. I can trust Ronan like I trusted Logan. He'll understand. "I'll tell you," I whisper.

"What?" His brow furrows and I realize he probably hadn't been able to hear me clearly with my head down.

"I'll tell you, Ronan. I'll tell you about what happened... before..."

His hand comes down on my shoulder. "You don't have to. It doesn't matter. All that matters, is I believe in you. I'm behind you one hundred percent and we are going to make this right, son."

My throat tightens. I'm about to embarrass myself and cry like a fucking baby. I look away and he pretends not to notice.

"So the next thing we need to do is…" Ronan is interrupted when the phone behind the bar starts to ring. "Who the hell is calling now?" he grumbles as he slides off the stool and goes to retrieve it.

I'm glad for the interruption as it gives me a few extra minutes to compose myself.

"The Crash. This is Ronan," he barks into the cordless phone. After a brief pause, he continues. "What? It's Sunday and we're closed! I shouldn't be getting a delivery!"

I look over at him as he paces in frustration.

"Fine! Give me one minute!" Ronan slams the phone down on the bar. "Idiots. There's a delivery truck at our back door. The driver has been knocking and we didn't hear him."

"Now?" I ask in surprise, looking over my shoulder in the direction of the back store room.

"Yeah! The guy on the phone swears they told us they would have to make Monday's delivery a day early this week, but no one told me. I've got to handle this. Just give me a minute. Don't go anywhere."

Ronan takes long strides with a fury on his face. I don't envy the poor delivery guy. Maybe it will be Pete. The one that flirted with Kinleigh. That thought actually cheers me up a little.

Out of habit, I slide around to the back of the bar and start cleaning up. I've only been gone a week and already things are out of order. After setting things right, I grab a bar towel and wipe down the counters. Soon, I start shooting glances toward the back. Ronan has been gone too long.

"Ronan?" I yell. Nothing. *How big is the delivery?*

I'm halfway across the bar when I hear a thud from above. Stopping, I look up and strain to hear more. I know Kinleigh isn't home. Ronan had told me when he called and convinced me to come over that she'd gone to visit her mom.

I take a few more steps when I hear a scream and I know it's her. *Kinleigh.*

Chapter Thirty-Three: Kinleigh
Please Don't Do This

My mom wasn't happy when I decided to cut our visit short, but she'd understood. After what I learned from Deanna, I needed to be home. I needed to be with Kyle and make him see that I'm by his side and we will make this right.

I pull my car into the parking lot behind The Crash, slipping my keys into the pocket of my jeans. I head for the stairs to my apartment with my bag. Mom had overnighted the extra car keys the day after Jeremy had attacked me, since my ring had never shown up, and I'm extra cautious about knowing where they are at all times now. I don't have the luxury of another backup set and having a new set made is expensive.

Halfway up the metal staircase, I notice behind my dad's car is Kyle's motorcycle. *Good.* I'm glad he's already here. The sooner we take care of this nonsense, the better!

Pulling back the heavy exterior door, I notice the hall is still pretty dark. I know Dad had replaced the bulbs as soon as I told him they were out, so we must have a short or a faulty breaker. Stepping forward into the gloom, I feel a chill. The hairs on my arm stand up. I've never been easily spooked, but something doesn't feel right.

"Dad? Kyle?" I call out, but there's no answer. "Is anyone there?" Again, silence. I take slow steps to close the distance to my apartment door. My last step is met by a soft resistance under my shoe. Bending down, I realize I've stepped on a flower. A single tulip. I drop my heavy bag and turn to run.

I'm not quick enough. My apartment door slides open and arms wrap around me, pulling me inside.

I scream, but a hand quickly clamps over my mouth to muffle me.

"Not another sound," Jeremy whispers hotly into my ear.

Dragging me backward, he uses his foot to kick the door closed behind us. I try to bite down on his hand, or struggle out of his vice-like grip but then feel a cold metal barrel pushed hard into my ribs. I go perfectly still. He has a gun.

"There's a good girl," he praises, finally pulling back his hand but still keeping his firm grip around my body. He starts to pet my hair and murmur sweet things about how beautiful I am and how he's missed me. I feel vomit trying to burn its way up my esophagus.

"Please," I beg. "Don't do this."

"You left me no choice." He removes the gun from my side and lets it caress the side of my cheek. My breath is coming in labored pants and it takes everything I have not to scream.

"Why? Why are you doing this?" I feel tears brimming over and blurring my vision.

"I told you. You just need time with me. I don't want to hurt

215

you and I won't... unless you leave me no choice. Just be a good girl. We will go and get in my car and take a little vacation together." He kisses the top of my head. "That's just what we need. Where would you like to go, baby? Anywhere you want."

"I don't..." I take a deep breath. "I don't want to go anywhere. Please."

"We just need to get away from your overprotective dad and that... that bartender, Kyle." He spits out the name like it contains poison. "You'll see. We will have a wonderful time. Maybe we can go somewhere tropical and work on our tans?"

I'm scared. I'm more scared than I've ever been. Having someone try to take you at gunpoint is a terrifying thing but realizing that person is insane is even scarier.

"But... before we go..." He turns me around and pushes me to the floor. "Maybe you need to give me a little taste of what you so willingly gave away to another."

Chapter Thirty-Four: Kyle
Don't Let Me Be Too Late

I take the steps two at a time and tear across the dark hallway to her apartment door.

Please, God... Don't let me be too late!

Kicking out, the door flies open and what I see horrifies me. Kinleigh is on her back on the floor, struggling. Jeremy is straddling her, trying to subdue her wrists above her head with one hand and ripping at her shirt with the other. I see he has a handgun stuck into the back waistband of his pants, but it doesn't even give me pause.

Flashbacks of my mom's ordeal register with lightning speed. She'd been struggling too. The bookie had ripped her favorite dress. My stepdad had been watching.

I don't scream out. I don't say a word. I lunge across the room, tackling Jeremy and propelling him off Kinleigh and into the coffee table. The sound of his head cracking against the heavy wooden leg brings me a shot of pure satisfaction, but it wasn't enough to knock him out. He manages to roll away and he's reaching behind him for the gun when I attack again. We roll across the floor together. I'm vaguely aware of Kinleigh's screaming, but it's just background noise at this point.

My hand finally finds its target. I squeeze hard on his throat while forcing the back of his head down onto the tile of the kitchen as hard as I can. I can tell I'm going to win. I can tell he is weakening.

Suddenly, there is a loud bang. It's even louder than Kinleigh's screaming. Everything goes dark.

Chapter Thirty-Five: Kinleigh
To Save Kyle, I'd Do It Again

"Ma'am. I need you to sit still and let me make sure you are okay."

Despite the doctor trying to take my blood pressure, I jump off the exam table and pull back the curtain, only to find a police officer guarding me from leaving.

"Please!" I beg him. "I have to know about Kyle! He was shot!"

He turns me back toward the doctor. "I know, Miss Walters. You get yourself checked out and I'll take you to the waiting room. Kyle Taylor is still in surgery."

"I'm fine! And I don't need an escort!"

The cop doesn't even flinch. "You let the doctor decide if you are fine. And for now, because of what happened... it is my job to stay with you."

I swallow hard and give in. *He's right. I guess I'm lucky I'm not in handcuffs right now.*

The doctor pulls the curtain back around us and finishes my exam. As I already knew, I'm fine, barring a few cuts and scrapes. Once dressed, I am led back to the third floor. In the cramped waiting room, occupying every tacky orange plastic chair, are all of Kyle's friends and family.

Liv and Zac are huddled together, cuddling Ben. Charli is feeding Jaci a bottle while Logan paces in front of her. Madison is wiping her eyes with a tissue while her boyfriend Mike rubs her back. The hardest scene to watch involves my dad and DeAnna. Kyle's mom looks like she's about to faint and my deathly pale father, with a large bandage wrapped around his head, is trying to comfort her.

"Daddy?" I croak out as I run forward and collapse into his arms.

"I'm fine, baby girl. Everything will be fine." He kisses the top of my head and I start to sob.

"Oh, Kinleigh. Thank you." DeAnna reaches over and takes my hands between hers. "You saved him."

"Did I?" I ask, doubtfully. "Is he going to make it?"

"Well..." she starts to tear up. "He's not out of surgery yet but... I have faith. My son is strong. He'll pull through."

I have to believe that too. The thought of a world without Kyle isn't bearable.

"How's your head, Dad?" I watch as he gingerly reaches up to pat his bandage.

"Fine. It will take more than a knock to the head to finish me."

"Kinleigh? Ronan?"

Turning to find my mother entering the waiting room brings relief and a fresh wave of tears. Her appearance also comes as a surprise to Dad and I watch him jump and scramble away from DeAnna.

"Amber?" Her name on his lips sounds more like a plea.

Wrapping one arm around me, she then pulls my dad in close too. He doesn't resist for long and for the first time in a long time, we feel like a family.

"Oh, baby," she croons near my ear. "I drove as fast as I could as soon as I heard." She reluctantly releases me and holds me out to inspect the damage. "Are you alright? Where does it hurt?"

"I'll be fine, Mom. I promise. I'm just worried about..." I choke, thinking of Kyle still in surgery and the uncertainty of what his future holds.

"I know. I'm so sorry." She turns to my father. "Ronan? Are you okay?" The concern is real and I watch, feeling like an intruder as they stare wordlessly for several seconds.

I clear my throat. "Mom?"

With the spell finally broken, she looks back at me. "Yes?"

Stepping to the side, I pull DeAnna forward. "This is DeAnna Taylor. DeAnna, this is my mom, Amber."

Mom's lips stiffen and she eyes the new acquaintance. "How nice to meet you." She looks over at Dad before continuing. "And you are...?"

"This is Kyle's mother," I explain.

Instant regret flits across my mom's face and all coldness vanishes. "Oh!" She pulls her into her arms and hugs tight. "Oh, DeAnna! I'm so sorry about Kyle! Kinleigh has told me so much about him and if he hadn't shown up when he did..." She starts to sob and the women cling to one another in shared fear and worry.

"Amber, thank you for your concern for my Kyle. I have to believe he will pull through. He's a good man and he did what was right. And Kinleigh's quick thinking gave him a real chance." DeAnna smiles at me. "You are a very special young lady, Kinleigh. Kyle cares so much for you… and so do I."

"Thank you. I feel the same."

We all find chairs and settle in, waiting for news on Kyle's condition. I'm sitting between my parents, but I notice them both looking at each other over my head on more than a few occasions. I'm feeling like the third wheel.

"Kinleigh…" Mom squeezes my hand. "Can you tell me about it?"

"Oh…" *Can I? Can I relive what happened last night?*

"Only if you can."

I think about the dark hallway outside my apartment and the feel of Jeremy's arms closing around me and start to feel sick. Mentally I skip ahead, after Kyle's arrival and the horrible events that followed. I just can't think about those things now.

Clearing my throat, I try to tell her what I can. "Jeremy…" I shudder with revulsion as I say his name. "He uh… He called the bar and pretended he was making a delivery so Dad would go to the back door. He had a tire iron and he ambushed him and…"

After everything, I'd called for an ambulance and when I'd heard the sirens and ran down to show them the way up to the apartment, I'd found my dad lying face down in a pool of blood near the back door. I thought he was dead. I'm convinced the only reason I still have my father is because Jeremy must have worried someone would hear the gunshot and ruin his plans to grab me.

"Ronan…" My mom's eyes sparkle with the promise of tears.

"I'm fine, Amber," he assures her, but his voice has lost its usual gruffness.

I'm about to try and tell them more when the door opens and

a petite nurse in blue scrubs walks in. Everyone in the room goes instantly silent and stands as we wait for news.

"He's out of surgery," she says with a smile and I feel a whoosh of breath leave me. "He's stable and in recovery. The bullet nicked several organs and exited near his spine. The next twenty-four hours are critical, but we have every reason to believe he will recover."

DeAnna falls back into the chair. "Oh, thank God," she whispers over and over again.

I clear my throat and step forward. "Can I see him?" I ask.

"Not yet. I'll let you know as soon as the doctor allows visitors." She smiles in sympathy and leaves us to comfort one another. When the door opens again a few minutes later, my dad steps in front of me before I can see who has joined us.

"Miss Taylor," the officer from earlier says as I peer around my hulking father. "Miss Taylor, we have to get your statement now. I know this is a hard time and I know it was self-defense but..."

"Are you charging my daughter with anything?" my dad asks, still standing between us.

"Not at this time, sir. As I said, we just need to get all the facts straight."

I put my hand on Dad's shoulder. "It's okay. I can talk to him."

"I also need you to understand that you can't leave this hospital for the time being."

I feel my dad tense. "I understand," I tell the officer. "I'm not going anywhere."

"If you can just follow me." He turns back to the door. I start to follow, but Logan jumps up and joins me.

"I'm her lawyer and I will be there during all questioning," he demands.

The officer sighs. "Fine. If you will both follow me."

Our shoes echo loudly on the faded linoleum as we are led into a small, private lounge. We sit down at a round table and the officer opens a large file.

"Can I get either of you a cup of coffee or bottle of water before we begin?" he asks politely.

"No, I'm fine," I assure him as Logan just shakes his head.

"Okay, then let's just go over the facts." He clasps his fingers together and puts them on top of the open file. "You called 9-1-1 at," he looks down and checks his notes, "7:34 this evening."

Logan nods at me so I answer. "Yes. I called from my cell phone while in my apartment."

The officer smiles, happy I'm being cooperative. "Okay, good. In the call, you stated that Jeremy Duncan had shot Kyle Taylor and you needed an ambulance."

"Yes."

"You also told the operator that Jeremy Duncan was dead."

I close my eyes and try to block the sight of him, lying on his back in a pool of his own blood. "Yes."

When the paramedics arrived on the scene, they confirmed Mr. Duncan was deceased, Mr. Taylor had been shot and needed emergency care, and your father," he checked his notes, "Ronan Walters, was unconscious from a blow to the head."

"Yes," I said again.

"You also admitted to the paramedics that you were the one to kill Mr. Duncan."

Logan puts a staying hand on my arm. "Are you charging my client?" he asks tensely.

"As I said before..." The officer's phone begins to ring loudly and I jump. He looks down at the number and frowns. "Excuse me. I need to take this." He steps out of the room and I let my shoulders sag.

"Logan." I turn to look at him. "I know you are helping me. I appreciate it. But I need to tell him what happened. It's pretty obvious anyway."

"Kinleigh, trust me. We aren't going to deny what you did, but there is a right way and a wrong way to admit to it."

"Well, that sounds ridiculous!" I jump out of the chair and pace around the stifling room. "I need to just..." I break off when the door opens back up and a different officer enters. He looks familiar.

"Miss Walters. I'm Detective Bradshaw. It's nice to see you again... although I'm sorry, it is under these circumstances."

Bradshaw... How do I know this man?

Suddenly I remember. He'd been the officer that Dad and I had spoken to after Kyle's arrest. He was the one to tell us about Kyle's earlier assault charges.

"Hello," I mumble, not sure if he is here to help or cause more problems.

"In light of new evidence, I want you to know you will not be charged with anything in connection with the death of Jeremy Duncan. All charges against Kyle Taylor in the assault case have also been dropped."

I sink back into my chair. "New evidence?" I ask incredulously.

He joins us at the table and reaches across to pat the back of my hand. "Yes, ma'am. We've discovered some things about Jeremy Duncan."

"What things?" Logan asks, kicking into lawyer mode again.

"Well, for starters... his name is really Jason McKade."

I'm not sure how to react to this revelation. "Jason?"

"Yes. Jason McKade was removed from his home, where he lived with his father, at the age of thirteen after a teacher saw signs of abuse. Jason wouldn't admit to anything and eventually he ended back in his father's house by the age of fifteen. He lived there until he finished high school and earned an academic scholarship to college. By all accounts, he did well in school, but then his father was involved in an accident at work over summer break and Jason had to go home to care for him. Before fall semester was to start back up, there was a house fire and his father died."

"Oh," I put my hand to my mouth, feeling sorry for the man I'd thought of as Jeremy. He'd told me he was close to his father and that must have been horrible for him. "Where was Jeremy... I mean Jason... when the house burned?"

"Well, he claimed he needed a break and had gone out to a local bar, but we could never get confirmation that he was there."

"Why would he lie?" I ask.

"The fire was a little suspicious. The local police officers had some doubts as to how it started, but there wasn't enough evidence to bring charges."

"Oh my God!" I feel sickness threatening. "You think he did it? He killed his own father?"

"I couldn't say for sure... but..." He lets the silence finish his thought.

"So his father dies. Then what?" I ask, scared to know more.

"Jason goes back to school and right before graduation a fellow student claims he is stalking her. He won't leave her alone and she's scared. He denies everything. A week later, she's been attacked by a masked assailant she swears is Jason. Again, he denies it and he's about to possibly get away with it until his lab partner comes forward and claims he attacked her too. Her roommate arrived in time to save her and wanted to report it, but the poor girl was scared to death and just wanted to get her degree and get the hell away from him. She stayed quiet until she heard about his new victim."

I had gone out with this man. I had been alone with him on numerous occasions. I'd almost been his next victim.

"Why wasn't he arrested?"

"He skipped town. We couldn't find him. That's when he must have changed his name and become Jeremy. He probably could have gone about his life, never answering for his past, except when his fingerprints were taken in the morgue..." He pauses when he notices me shudder at the word. "when his prints were taken here at the hospital and put in the system, it pinged the old cases."

I start to cry. The stress over Kyle's condition, worrying about my dad, and most of all... the realization that I had taken another person's life all crash in on me.

"I stabbed him," I whisper. "He was fighting with Kyle. Kyle had come to save me and he was going to die because of it." I gulp in a ragged gasp of air. "I didn't know what to do! I grabbed the big chef's knife I keep on my kitchen counter, the one with the pink handle that my mom bought me..." I know I'm babbling, but once the floodgates open, there's no stopping me. "Kyle was choking him. I thought... I thought it would be okay. Jeremy would pass out. We could call the police. But then..."

Logan puts his arm around me and squeezes lightly. "You had to, Kinleigh."

I brush him off. "Jeremy grabbed his gun. It was in the back of his pants and he grabbed it and... It was so loud. Kyle's shirt started turning red. It kept spreading. Bigger and bigger and bigger..."

"Kinleigh..." Logan pleads, but I have to get it out. The story is poisoning me.

"So much blood. I thought... I thought..."

"It's okay, Miss Walters. It was self-defense. You were scared he would turn on you with the gun and you were right to believe that," Detective Bradshaw tells me.

"No!" I jump up and go over to a small window, overlooking the hospital parking lot. "I didn't," I tell them with my back to them all. "I never thought about him shooting me. I just thought if he pulls that trigger again... I'll lose Kyle for sure. So before he could, I..."

"Kinleigh!" Logan's voice sounds distant and I feel myself starting to waver. I need to sit down.

I had killed a man. And to save Kyle, I'd do it again.

Chapter Thirty-Six: Kyle

Blissful, Dark Silence

It's dark. All dark. Everywhere dark. Until it isn't.

There's brightness trying to penetrate my eyelids. I fight it.

It is quiet. Pure silence. Until there is sound.

An electronic beeping intrudes. I want it to stop.

I feel nothing. I'm disconnected and floating and everything is calm. Until it isn't.

Pain explodes through my chest and I can't escape it.

I hear voices. Muffled and confusing. I try to understand what they're saying, but it's hard. I know the words, but their meaning is lost to me.

"...his blood pressure is spiking..."

"...he's lost so much blood..."

"...thank God it missed his spine..."

"...I think he's coming out of it... No, Mr. Taylor... don't fight us..."

"...give him another dose..."

And then the blissful, dark, silence descends again.

Chapter Thirty-Seven: Kyle
Say It Again

"Kyle?"

I know her voice. She's worth waking up for.

"Kyle? Can you hear me?"

"Kinleigh?" My throat explodes in pain as I say her name.

"Shhhh..." I feel her stroking back my hair and squeezing my hand.

"What happened?" I whisper, scared to talk any louder and praying she can hear me.

"Everything is going to be okay. I promise. You just rest."

My thoughts are blurring in and out. There is something I need to remember. Something important. Something about Kinleigh."

Jeremy!

I open my eyes and jerk up, pulling at all the tubes and connections, needing to get away. Needing to protect Kinleigh!

"Nurse!" Kinleigh yells while practically laying on top of me. A door opens and a tall woman in bright blue scrubs runs over, pulling a glass bottle from her pocket.

"Mr. Taylor, calm down," she pleads. "I can help with the pain but…"

"Fuck the pain!" I yell, letting fire rip through my throat. "He wants to hurt her!"

"Kyle!"

I turn my head and see Ronan and my mom standing in the open doorway. I relax. Ronan will help me. He'll never let Jeremy get Kinleigh.

"Save her," I plead. "Don't let him hurt her!"

"Never," Ronan promises and I believe him. I slip back into the dark.

I have no idea how long I'm gone, but once again sights and sounds are making themselves known. Kinleigh is asleep in the chair next to my bed, with her hand stuck through the railing and gripped in mine.

"Hey, Princess," I say softly, testing my limits. She stirs immediately.

"Kyle!" She jumps up and kisses my forehead. Then she starts to sob.

Now I am the one shushing her. "Don't cry, baby. I'm fine. Really." I don't want to admit my chest feels like someone stuck a red-hot poker through its center.

"Oh my God, Kyle. I thought I lost you!"

"Never," I assure her.

"You were shot. I thought…"

I tense at her words, remembering the sound the gun had made and the pain that had followed. I can't remember anything more.

"What happened?" I ask her.

She looks away.

"Kinleigh?" I use the hand not connected to the IV to grab her chin and turn her face back to mine. "What happened?"

I spend the next half hour in total shock as she relates the rest of the story. Apparently, I had rushed in to save her and by the time it was over, she ended up saving me.

I hold her against me, ignoring the pain, as she cries out her fears, her regrets, and the loss of part of herself she should never have lost.

"Do you have any idea how much I love you?" I ask when the tears finally dry up.

Her head jerks up in shock. "You've never... I mean I knew but... You've never said it and..."

"I'm sorry. I should have. I should have told you every hour of every day since I first realized it."

"Say it again," she begs and I laugh.

"I love you."

"I love you too."

Epilogue: Ronan

"This thing will end up starting late," I grumble.

"No, it won't!" Kinleigh assures me.

"These things always start late," I insist as I adjust the buttons that run a perfect line down the front of my jacket. It's a little snug nowadays, but I'm proud I can still fit in the dress uniform I'd worn to my retirement party.

"Daddy, you look so handsome." Kinleigh's praise makes it hard to keep it together. I'm so damn proud of her and she looks so beautiful in her lacy dress with flowers pinned in her hair.

How am I going to keep from crying today?

The thick wooden door behind us groans loudly as Liv and Charli join us. They are both dressed in their Sunday best and I'll admit I'm damn proud of them too.

"Wow. You guys look great!" Charli tells me as she lifts her toddler up to give me a kiss on the cheek.

"Pwetty Wonan!" Jaci squeals before jumping out of her

234

mother's arms to run behind a very pregnant Liv to pull out the hiding Ben.

No longer chubby, the tall spindly-legged boy is shy and tries pushing her away.

How in the hell had Liv, of all people, ended up with a shy kid?

"Ben!" Liv pulls him forward. "Tell your Auntie Kinleigh and Ronan how nice they look." He just closes his eyes and pretends we don't exist.

I squat down until we see eye to eye. "Benjamin. It's time to grow up and quit hiding behind your Momma's skirts! You're about to be a big brother and almost a man now."

One eye opens and he looks at me skeptically. "I am?" he whispers.

"Absolutely. Don't let these women run roughshod over you! Stand up for yourself!"

He takes a minute to contemplate my advice. "Yes, sir. I will."

There may be hope for him yet.

"Me too! Me too!" Jaci yells while twirling in circles and letting her dress fan out. "I'm a man! I'm a man!"

I turn to correct her, but Kinleigh puts a hand on my arm to stop me. "It's pointless, Dad. She is determined to do and say everything Ben does. Haven't you figured out yet how strong-willed the women in your life are?"

I grunt but concede the point.

"We just wanted to pop in and wish you luck and congratulations again. See you out front!" Charli says and she and Liv herd the kids back out of the room to join the rest of the guests.

Finally alone, I have one more thing I need to discuss with Kinleigh before this ceremony begins.

I pull an envelope from my pocket and hand it to her. "Here. I want you and Kyle to have this."

She frowns. "What is it?"

"Just open the damn envelope and see!"

She laughs, but unseals it and pulls out a thick stack of papers. "I don't understand."

"What's not to understand? I'm tired of dealing with the bar. I want out."

"Daddy, you love that bar and..."

"Let a man talk!" I insist. "Logan drew up the papers. You and Kyle get the bar. I've also liquidated some assets I didn't need any more and I've had an architect draw up some plans to turn the upstairs into your cupcake bakery. It's my wedding gift to you both."

Tears start falling down her cheeks and she leans forward to kiss my cheek. "Thank you, Daddy! It's too much. You didn't have to!"

"I know I didn't. I wanted to."

"But," she looks confused again. "Why today? Why would you give me my wedding gift today when our wedding is still six months away?"

"Well..." I clear my throat. "Amber... I mean... your mom and I talked it over. We've spent enough time apart in our lives. After this *thing* today makes us officially together again, I'm moving back home with her. It's time for the young people to work hard and let us enjoy our retirement."

The sound of the organ gives us our cue. It's time to go out there and officially give up my bachelor status once and for all.

The End

About The Authors

Once upon a time, these two hookers became best friends...

Stacey Brandon and Karen Bell both live in the same small Texas town on the Gulf Coast, are happily married and the proud Moms of awesome kids. Stacey owns and runs a photography studio and Karen designs and sews her own children's clothing line. They met over fifteen years ago when they decided to turn one large professional space into a single home for both businesses.

Well, that's all the boring facts expected to be included in an "about the author" page, right? The reality is so much more fun. Stacey and Karen and their families spend holidays together, travel together... and generally turn every situation into something crazy and chaotic. They are both fluent in English, Sarcasm and Profanity and have decided the irrefutable proof of their best friend status is how often people assume they are "together" when in public. The poor husbands are good sports about it... and might even encourage this misconception at times for sheer entertainment value.

When Karen battled cancer... and kicked its ass... in 2014, they learned to value every day and quit worrying about what others think. Do what you love! Karen is happy to take advantage of the situation though. She loves to remind everyone she "had the CANCER, dammit!" and now she can always and forever claim the last brownie ;)

Stacey Brandon

Karen Bell

Acknowledgements

From Stacey:

As Always, I want to acknowledge the love and support I receive from my husband, Calvin. No matter what I want to do, where I want to go, or what crazy plan I concoct – he's on board 110%. This would never have happened without someone like him backing me up. And to our children and grandchildren (whether it be by birth, marriage, or plain luck) ... you guys are everything to me. I love you more than you know: Justin, Krysten, Kayla, Ronnie, Steven, Hannah, Carson, Easton, and Brixton.

From Karen:

My dearest "Donward" – You make me understand what they mean by soul mate. It was always you and it will always be you. I love you beyond reason. And I can't forget to send all my love and thanks to my sons – Shawn and Tyler. They are instrumental in making theses books happen and I am the proudest mom ever.

From Stacey & Karen:

Amber Byford, DeAnna 'Juicy D' Ben, and Carol West... our "Book Girls" – you give us ideas, honest feedback, unending support, and most of all *Laughter*. We love you.

To Laura Hampton, the best editor and one of our biggest cheer-leader. You rock ;)

Thanks to Donnie Bell for constantly reminding us we need to write and quit playing around, and all the awesome line editing he does during his time off from his real job. Love you!

Tyler Bell – We love you for saving our butts constantly with your mad computer skills!

Crash Series:

Crash

Fall

Wreck

Continue Reading

For the Synopsis of

Crash and Fall - The books that

started it all...

Crash

Stacey Brandon & Karen Bell

Charli has a plan for her life. It does not include the hot guy at table four. This is the first time she's seen him at *The Crash*, the bar where she works most evenings. From the moment he arrives with his condescending friends, power suit and unnerving stare... he's hijacked her thoughts. It doesn't help that he keeps finding ways to insinuate himself into her life.

Logan has a plan for his life. It does not include the quirky little waitress at the new bar his friends discovered. He has a lot of obligations and very little time. If he needs a female distraction once in awhile, she isn't the type of woman he normally turns to. Despite all of this, she has become what he wants most of all.

Working to overcome all the things threatening to separate them won't be easy. Can they find a way to meet in the middle if it holds the promise of happily ever after?

Fall

Stacey Brandon & Karen Bell

Liv is smart, sexy, and confident. Just ask her. She isn't shy. Her photography business is starting to really take off, she has amazing friends, and there has never been a shortage of boyfriends. With so much to offer, why hasn't she ever fallen in love?

Zac followed his dream and just opened his first restaurant. He is also about to marry the woman he has loved since he was in high school. He has his life right on track and couldn't be happier.

When Liv is hired to photograph Zac's upcoming wedding, she realizes why she's never been in love before... She hadn't met the right guy yet.

When Zac gets to know the photographer for his wedding, he can't stop thinking about her. It doesn't change his love for his fiance'... but Liv fascinates him and that scares him more than he wants to admit.

What happens when you fall for a guy that already belongs to someone else?

Stay "In The Know"

FACEBOOK:
https://www.facebook.com/BrandonBell.Authors/

INSTAGRAM:
brandon_bell_authors

WEBSITE:
www.BrandonBellAuthors.com

Email:
BrandonBell.Authors@gmail.com